ALBERT'S JOURNAL OF THE UNIVERSE

...tim; plummer...

Copyright © 2023 ...tim; plummer....

All rights reserved. No part of this book may be reproduced, stored, or transmitted by any means—whether auditory, graphic, mechanical, or electronic—without written permission of both publisher and author, except in the case of brief excerpts used in critical articles and reviews. Unauthorized reproduction of any part of this work is illegal and is punishable by law.

ISBN: 979-8-89031-249-5 (sc)
ISBN: 979-8-89031-250-1 (hc)
ISBN: 979-8-89031-251-8 (e)

Because of the dynamic nature of the Internet, any web addresses or links contained in this book may have changed since publication and may no longer be valid. The views expressed in this work are solely those of the author and do not necessarily reflect the views of the publisher, and the publisher hereby disclaims any responsibility for them.

One Galleria Blvd., Suite 1900, Metairie, LA 70001
1-888-421-2397

CONTENTS

RECAP OF ALBERT'S JOURNEY ix

1st entry	DREAMING REALITY INTO EXISTENCE	1
2nd entry	DOGMA UPRISING	13
3rd entry	COSMIC MOVIE	22
4th entry	SOURCE WHISPERER	32
5th entry	SOUND VIBRATIONS	42
6th entry	CONCEPTUAL LOSS	51
7th entry	A DYNAMIC SHIFT	59
8th entry	ART AS A MEDIUM FOR REALITY	69
9th entry	FIRST CONTACT	77
10th entry	MISSION REPORT	87
11th entry	DREAM A LITTLE DREAM OF ME	99
12th entry	LIFE IN AN ALTERNATE REALITY	109
13th entry	VISIONS OF ENLIGHTENED SOCIETY	120
14th entry	DEBT AS SLAVERY	131
15th entry	COSMIC PARADIGM TRANSFORMATION	141
16th entry	UNSUPPORTED VALIDATION	151
17th entry	TRANSFORMATION EXPECTATION	163
18th entry	DREAM AWAKENING	173

Welcome to a better reality of imagination, one that has overcome many of man's pointless self-inflicted illnesses. The change began with the children, the education system went from schooling centers to learning centers. One's learning never stops, there is no twelve grades. To graduate is to choose your passions, exploring known past knowledge to further develop your skills and natural abilities. Graduation is a gradual lifelong, never-ending progress, not a final accomplishment. Information is readily available to all, not just chosen, select, edited, refined or bias information either. The first rule of Natural Law (DO NO HARM) is explored in all aspects, accounting for cause and effect. Reading, writing, language, math along with Natural Law are required and integrated into all learning processes.

Bringing value to existence is each one's competition with themselves. Productive time is the new currency that is measured into credits that are shared to redeem precious time from others. Time learning, time caring for others, time cleaning your surroundings, time traveling, and every second has a value. This value belongs to everyone, not some government, religion or State. Working a job is now called, "bringing a value".

With a portion of this story I took many liberties (all public info) with creating a version of Earths his/her-story using names/words/actors/concepts that may be familiar. I claim no secret knowledge or accuracy but search for answers on how man is a captive of our own self-created reality. This is written with levity as our choices are what bring us this funny/not-funny existence. Imagining a better world is a great start in creating one.

One other liberty I took was with language. I attempt to explain the verbiage used as the story progresses. All this is just fun in the playground.

Language is a double-edged sword, capturing/limiting our collective view of the universe, it is also a tool for creation and comprehension. Unless we become telepathic or empaths, we need words as our neural path to each other, in this global mind. Language could be like math where one is always one and one plus two is always three. No wonder other advanced beings in the universe may feel that man is primitive, in many ways we speak and understand gibberish. I share my gibberish with anyone who reads this alternate reality. Just have fun!

The scene for this story is just fifteen years from now in our calendar timestream. In a cone of possibilities/probabilities, the further into the future, probabilities are greater and less predictable. If we choose to make value our higher go-all, this garden planet can blossom.

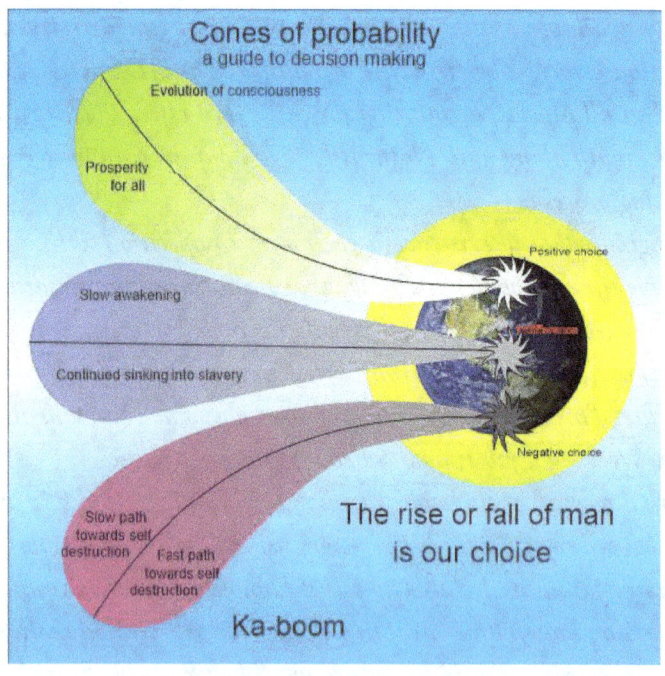

Albert has made it his life decision to follow the positive timestream, duh! It only makes sense!!! It became a global choice to follow the obvious positive timeline creating a reality of not only survival but true prosperity.

Join us in a story that is created from the positive timeline where your decisions played a role in cause and effect. We are on this ride together. You are a player in this new story line, welcome!!!

RECAP OF ALBERT'S JOURNEY

As you read the story remember your child within. The cast of characters from "Albert's Journey into the Universe" link together in a shared dream. In one day they explore the multi-verse, Omni-verse, micro-verse, macro-verse, millions of years and many far out places. In a search for rest along with answers on how to maintain a healthy world. This story takes place after we (planet Earth and man) have achieved cosmic acceptance, clinging on to a golden age. You may have to read "Albert's Journey into the Universe" to find out how man got to this higher stage of being.

Re-introduction of characters starts with Albert who has tuned his time/space ability allowing him to mentally witness any place or time as if he was there. Nowhere or no-when is out of reach of his ability.

Albert's wife "Mary" (the group telepath) not only reads minds but can link minds to share common experiences. Tapping into the consciousness tapestry is maybe a better description of her ability.

Brandon's (Albert and Mary's oldest child) ability is language/communication. He is like a universal translator with the added application of conscious transference that allows for interaction of species.

Penny (the middle child) is mastering her ability to shape sound/frequency/vibration, matching the sound/frequency/vibration that make up anything or everything. Tuning into any verse of the universe, she sings shapes and form into existence.

Charles (the youngest) plays with molecules like logo blocks, tapping into the ether for the elements of creation. His childlike mind makes just about anything possible. Together the children are truly amazing.

Myra (the family's oldest and dearest friend) is a healer. Recognizing then removing illness just by giving needed nutrition, in many cases. Everything flourishes as she spots then corrects ailments.

Bill (Albert's lab partner and best friend) never stops searching for new perspectives of observation. Where most see just a tree, Bill sees the tree from every conceivable angle from the micro to the macro, in different spectrums, with a thirst for greater comprehension he places no limits on anything.

Seth is a new member of the group. He also gained enhanced natural essence abilities from the "Gateway's World Tour". Seth is a shapeshifter shaman that felt at home with this soul group.

Adrian Adams is Chief Executive of U.S.E. enterprises where Albert and Bill play at learning as scientist. She orchestrates many, if not all projects at U.S.E (Universal Space Exploration). One might say that her ability is recognizing, shaping and sharing value.

Zeb is Albert's multi-dimensional friend and guide. He manifests into a corporal form to interact with his friends. His luminescent form contains the vastness of our universe modeling a humanoid. He says that man is made in the image of the universe.

"I Am" as you may recall from the Gateway World tour is from the Andromeda Galaxy. He is also a multi-dimensional being, millions of years old who chooses to stay a child. He playfully became "The Gateway" to help mankind reach new levels on our path.

Scout is chosen leader of the mice, whose bravery has set into motion a leap in evolution among the rodent species. His experiences have taught him logic that continually surprises even the wisest of men.

Jasmine loves her leader, Scout quickly becoming his lifelong partner with an unspoken bond of trust, loyalty and common interest.

Runner, Cheezer, and Babbler are also part of Scout's tribe of mice. They love going on adventures with the hue-mans, in this venture they would truly be hues of man.

ALBERT'S JOURNAL OF THE UNIVERSE

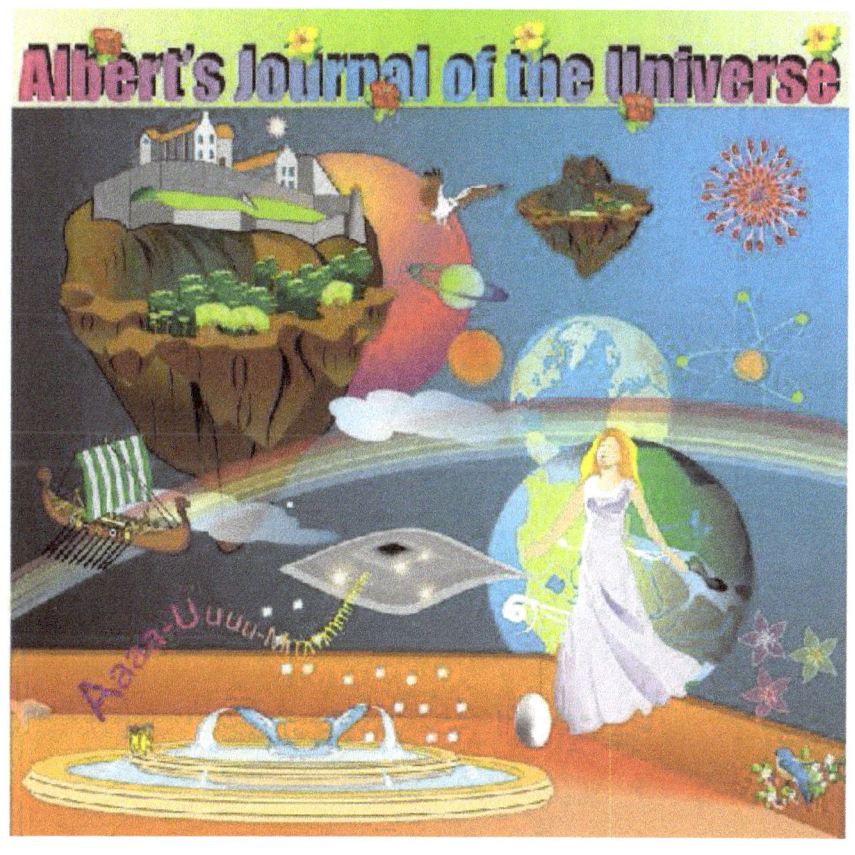

ALBERT'S JOURNAL OF THE UNIVERSE

1ST ENTRY

DREAMING REALITY INTO EXISTENCE

In all our known/unknown reality there is evidence that everything is one. Some call this entanglement, a web of co-existence. All of time and space exist in the here and now. We (all things) have been here since the beginning of creation in one form or another. Within this mage-ical (a mage is a seer) existence is a consciousness that continually seeks to discover itself. Each particle has its' own unique perspective. In this incredibly vast universe, some push the envelope of their limited perspective to further understand what some call source.

Diving into unexplored realms of conscious being with fearless wonder is a small cluster of physical neurons that make up the main characters of this story. Pushing the boundaries of know-ledge, tapping the dome of limitations is where this story begins. A record of their experiences is scripted then shared by a carbon-based neuron we know as "Albert".

Albert, along with his gifted family and friends have played roles in this cosmic play that has expanded man-kinds consciousness, bringing about a new path towards awareness. Only a small fraction of source consciousness has reached the higher elevations of perspectives that this group has. Albert provides an archive of events they experience, to be shared with the world mind then placed in the akashic records.

September 2nd-2045

Last night, in a restless slumber, I had a dream that my sub conscious mind must have drawn me to. What I mean by that is my conscious mind would not have chosen the intent that guided me in that dream scape. When these dreams occur we may have to question our sub conscious mind the purpose for these dream visions. The dream seems to be totally unrelated to the events happening or the questions we are seeking answers to.

One discipline that is used to gain awareness and control over the choices made while in the dream state is to become aware of yourself in your dream. Feel your vessel or hold your hands out to look at them (lucid dreaming). When I attempted to do this I discovered that I was a photon of light with no defining vessel or container. This fits into what I already feel to be truth, acceptance set in as I progressed along. I quickly noticed that there were photons all around that were gathering to form a beam of light heading in one direction. Some of the photons were very dim, almost extinguished as others were brighter than miniature stars. As the photons gathered they formed a light that could illuminate a vast amount of the visible universe.

All the photons were heading towards one source but at the end of the beam was source looking back at itself, looking to see if source could master the dream it was having. Source then looped the beam of photon back towards itself forming an infinity wave, then became that wave.

Now we get to the strange part of my dream. I could feel like I was an extremely bright photon that had my own path to source. As I attempted to join this infinity wave I kept coming against obstacles blocking my entrance to the source infinity wave. These were silly obstacles that one would think that they should be easy to overcome, especially in the powerful dreamscape where everything is possible. Electrical wires tangled me up, and then paper currency gagged my breath. How could this happen? I was a photon that did not need to breath. A struggle set in as I freed myself from these, but they gave the illusion that source was now almost out of reach.

As I headed back in what I felt was the direction of source I came across even more obstacles. Many of these new obstacles obviously came from within but others were apparent outward obstacles. Doubt, unworthiness and fear became my inner obstacles which I analyzed then dismissed or detached from them. I knew I was heading in the right direction but was  not totally sure. Distractions seemed to come from all directions. My comfort levels were being challenged as severe temperatures seemed to take over. I am a photon and these things do not matter, why was I letting this have any affect? Maybe I should just wake up? Maybe I should return to my warm bed next to my beautiful wife?

Small spasms of frustration appeared then disappeared. I remembered the beginning of my dream where all the other photons were shown to look within or back at themselves to find source. I stopped all the struggles then took just a moment away from the turmoil I chose to just be. Instantly I was back at the source infinity wave. Relief set in as I realized I had never left but I was experiencing another way for source to realize itself. I was offering my unique perspective.

Upon reaching source, I realized that I could transform myself into a Neuron (thought or brain wave). This allowed many abilities that even a photon could not achieve. As a Neuron, one can go anywhere in an instant, so linier time and space only existed if you choose to use the continuum. The only limitation was one can only enter places that are receptive or tuned in.

This existence was a wonderful realm that could be shaped, formed and reformed. It takes many Neuron to manifest something to our (prime Existence) so any Neuron has the challenge of finding receptors. As a Neuron, one is both a transmitter and a receiver, bringing in as much as it shares. Although it does not take validation from other Neuron for Truth to exist.

My first experience as a Neuron was to share the journey of being a photon along with the transformation into a Neuron. Finding other Neurons that were receptive was at first a struggle. The more receptive Neurons quickly tuned in. As they received information, they transmitted it to others.

It became clear that this story sharing had to be transformed into another dimension for further sharing, so upon waking my intent to write my dream experience down was paramount.

I woke up next to Mary (my lovely telepathic soul mate) who told me she shared my dream. This was not a typical dream for either of us. We both felt that we had overcome the learned behaviors of our early years and these were just fragments of our past paradigm.

Mary went on saying; "our struggles are like the common flu. Your body fights off the germ and builds immunity to it. Every so often this virus tries to take over again and our body knows how to handle it. It reminds us that we are lacking what our body may need. We may be free from dis-ease* but maybe it is because when we see the signs of dis-ease we know what to do".

After a moment, Mary continued; "We can go anywhere we chose on your vision journeys. We just have to define our intent. Let's get everyone together for a vacation journey where our intents are only to have fun. That should be a magical experience".

I asked where we might go. After all we should all be together. We do not want Charles going to some remote corner of the cosmos and getting lost. Mary contacted the entire team mentally to get an idea where everyone wanted to go. Mary's abilities have developed quite a bit, just like they have with the rest of us. She does not need a phone or technology to converse with anyone/anywhere. She can create a group link also without the limitation of distance or density. You could be visiting middle Earth "Agartha" and she could still make that communication link.

It was a unanimous decision to visit "I am" in ancient Lumeria again, with this new intent of having fun. We all met at the USE building for lunch before beginning our vision vacation. There was a vibration of calm excitement present as we headed towards the lab.

With the friends all gathered, Albert gave an itinerary; As far as we know, nothing like this has ever been done, creating a group mind for a 24-hour period with each participant keeping their unique individual spirit, perspective, personality, intent and destiny. For this to work we must all agree to always stay linked to the spirit family/group. The exploration of our inner- verse has shown us the universe and beyond.

Adrian (friend and C.E.O. of USE science foundation) has agreed to monitor our dream vacation using Halo projectors placed on our foreheads. The halo connects with brain waves then projects holographic images, the results of having this group link projecting into a common image will be a new experience.

All our journeys are videotaped in the lab where many surprising events have been discovered. Each camera is recording at different spectrums that are out of most people's normal senses. Many people have developed heightened senses after the Gateway's tour but cameras are still used for recording and archiving events. This is still recognized as the scientific way of verifying occurrences for the few remaining skeptics. Our recordings are also viewed in many classrooms everywhere.

The recordings from today's vacation vision journey will hold special significance to the archives and anyone stuck on logic. I have always felt that it is good to be logical but not good to be stuck on logic. Playing in a cosmic playground cannot be accomplished with a logical mind. This dream experience will give us a chance to test suspended sleep intended to be used in space travel. We will know the significance of the recordings after the dream vacation.

It took the rest of the day to prepare for our inner journey. Everything was done with great excitement anticipating a playful romp in a mind garden.

We formed a close circle with the group, laying down on a round bed, we all got as comfortable as we could. The Halo projectors were placed on everyone and aligned the projection beam with a common focal point in the center of the room. We focused on the intent of having fun and playing at what we loved the most. This would be a two week vacation that lasted for hundreds of lifetimes, billions of years in one afternoon. Try to keep up with us if you have a logical mind.

Mary linked all our minds and it was like we all got into the same vehicle or vessel and I was the driver that would take us all to our dream vacation. To Lamuria. I felt like a child, full of energy and excitement; we all did! Our trip took about three seconds as we arrived in Lemuria.

"I am" and Zeb are there to greet us. They have chosen this place and time as home. Being with them in their comfort zone brought about a feeling of calm serenity. Creation was happening all around us, changes occurred moment to moment with every creature imaginable in abundance.

Energy filled the air as we saw new creations. You could not stop this joyous feeling that could bring you to all out laughter if you let it. Most of us, (including the mice that were with us) laughed until tears poured out our eyes. Each tear fell to the ground then formed the landscape for our playground. For each of us it would be unique. Penny; with her wonderful imagination brought about trees, mountains, waterfalls, animals and lagoons along with playful characters one could only imagine in a story.

The tears of laughter from Charles created what is best described as cosmic toys. He created magical devises that would allow him to create at a whim whatever brought him joy. This was Charles ability already (to create out of thin air with the molecules around) but if was now instantaneous. One of his toys was a video screen that he manifested in front of him that transported him to any insight location on the screen. He could channel any location with his screen. This line of sight transporter was not really necessary for travel but it provided Charles with great entertainment. I did not know that he would or could bring these toys back with him from our vision vacation. Children are full of surprises. He was quickly becoming the master of molecules'; so nothing should surprise me. He walks through the air as if walking on land. It is not telekinesis he is using as much as it is a collaboration he has with the molecules or field around him. Maybe that is what being telekinetic is all about but it is more with Charles; he can now pull molecules together out of the air to make objects. He does not need tears of laughter to help him create.

Mary's tears created a beautiful beach with wonderful rock formations and a large natural cliff along the beach. All the elements were there for her to enjoy. She played in the ocean of her imagination then frolicked in the sands of timelessness, building sand castles of extreme beauty then witnessed them get washed away by the erosion that the ocean water caused when a large wave came in. She giggled like a small child that was just letting go.

Bill, the groups observer, created geometric worlds that he could explore in detail. He now has control when he goes exploring, so he always knows his way back from anywhere. He simply returns to his heart center where all his love ones are and he returns automatically to rejoin the group. His tears created an entire galaxy but it fit into the dreamscape perfectly. We would only see Bill once in a while as he blinked in and out of our present reality. He was like a playful pixie or pixel of light darting from place to place, exploring everything.

Myra, well known for her healing ability, cried tears of nourishment that brought vibrant heath to everything. She was now in a place where there was no dis-ease and she could fully rest in comfort. For this vacation she was putting her concerns on the shelf with care to just be. Let the world do without her for just a little while. Myra's happiness was in a calm pool of relaxation where she could explore her universe detached from any obligations or distractions of any kind. This is where she creates the best. Her unique universe is one that is a relished perspective to the GREAT I AM, bringing exuberant health to all that is.

Albert's Journal of the Universe

Each member of the team created their own perspective of paradise. The mice created a wonderful world of tunnels they could run through that had cheese snacks whenever they wanted them.

Out of all the mice it was Scouts dream reality that struck me the most. Scouts tears of laughter created a remote spot for just him and Jasmine. What was amazing was that Jasmine made the same spot as their tears pooled together. They would spend this vacation time dancing, playing and singing together without a worry of the tribe's needs or wants. Seeing two beings sharing the same passion is like watching the natural spring of life. You could see their unborn children in their eyes. Could Jasmine conceive life with Scout on a vision journey? We may find out!

Our new friend Seth shape shifted to all his totem animals then many more. First he was eagle, then he became python, hummingbird, jaguar, dolphin and some other beings we have only had visions of in our journeys. His tears of laughter created a dreamscape that only someone with the ability to experience life from so any realities could imagine. It was a reality full of wonders that excite all the senses. As eagle he saw everyone's dreamscape as one picture. He was able to become part of the multi-dimensional time/space that this hologram was being created in and see even the slightest movement or change. As dolphin he swam in the oceans of Mary's dreamscape. As hummingbird he went exploring with Bill. As inchworm he played with Charles who laughed with glee at Seth's new incarnation.

I was drawn back to my dream of being a photon. As a photon I spent most of my vacation visiting all of the team as they played in this cosmic playground. I could assume the form of my Albert vessel with just a thought. Mary joined me as a photon herself on many occasions. We all found that becoming a photon had many advantages. There was no strife here in this vision, as fun and relaxation was our full intent.

It was obvious we weren't in Lumeria any longer. Both "I am" and Zeb just observed our playground as if they took pleasure in our activities without partaking in them. What we conceived of as linear time showed up as evening time where we gathered and rested. We created an even bigger paradox in what some might consider a sub dream scape. This is where you see yourself having a dream in your dream. This may be confusing to some. We experienced two weeks of linear time on our vacation but back at the lab in the USE building we were only gone for twenty-four hours. To further confuse the reader of this journal I have to tell you that on the second day of our journey vacation some of us went hiking through timelines. It can be pretty confusing if you use a logical mind.

We went billions of years on our hike and it is hard to put into words what we saw on this hike. First off; time effects space so in order to even know that you are traveling through time is to associate it to as specific space. We chose the space to be the Andromeda Galaxy even though we had already witnessed billions of years on our visit with "I am". The galaxy is huge so we wanted to return.

Seth came with us as wolf to help keep tabs on Brandon, Charles and Penny. We had to stay together on the path. This was a family outing. Seth had his own mini universe to explore but chose to take time for this galactic hike. This would be a research mission.

Our first outlook was the planet Creton in the solar system Boulregard surrounded by the Petri nebula. Creton was rich with life that had always bathed in the waves pulsing through the nebula. We watched hundreds of species evolve, develop into light beings and begin their experiences with source. It was miraculous to witness light beings rise up off a planet to ascend into the stars.

Next we were on the planet Aquaticus of the solar system Origin. This overlook took us right into the habitat of a species called Merman.

We saw underwater cities that dazzle the imagination. The Mermen lived in unison with a highly evolved race that had long ago reached the realm of fifth dimensional existence. These beings are called the Illuminates. They chose to stay on Aquaticus as they loved the planet as the mother of their creation. The history between the two species went back millions of years and the relationship was not always peaceful co-existence.

The Illuminates are like jelly fish, they did not have or need a humanoid form. The ability to enter other beings' consciousness was a natural sense for them. They tapped into cosmic consciousness and received awareness of source in earlier development. It was strictly entertainment to have the Mermen build structures of exquisite beauty to please their optical senses. Placing ideas into the mind of the Mermen, making them unwitting slaves, playthings for the Illuminates. The Mermen benefitted by living and upkeeping the wonder they thought they created.

In the ancient time of Aquaticus some of the Illuminates felt that the Merman was there to serve them as they felt that they were the obvious superior being. For hundreds if not a thousand years this forced servitude was inflicted on the Merman. This paradigm passed as the Illuminates came to realize that the Merman was just another aspect of them that realized source creation on levels they had long ago detached from. In many ways the Merman was the superior species having potential that the Illuminatus may never achieve. Things changed from a position of control to one of jealousy. Even evolved beings can have petty emotions that have to be worked on. This was quickly put into perspective as they agreed to help each other to create what neither of them could create on their own.

...tim; plummer...

The Illuminates began embodying the technology being created by the Merman and would at some point explore the stars as galactic vessels for the Merman.

We saw many more planets along the trail that all have stories that we will share. Most of us were very tired after this cosmic hike and rested well that evening. We all agreed to go exploring in Seth's playground after our rest. Mary and I spent the dream evening on her beautiful beach under a display of stars matching any celestial background we had ever seen.

ALBERT'S JOURNAL OF THE UNIVERSE

2ND ENTRY

DOGMA UPRISING

September 2nd-2045
Continued

The next day came quickly with the group well rested. They met at the dream dawn to see who would join them in exploring Seth's mini universe. Bill and Myra would join Seth, Mary, Brandon, Penny, Charles and I on this sojourn. All of us agreed to go exploring as photons. The whole team has adapted to being and transforming into photons in this vision vacation. It was less restrictive when traveling about a five dimensional landscape.

We began our journey with Seth by following him to a small planet much like Earth. It only made sense that our creations would hold or form the reality we have come to know. Our memories were templates that were manifested into our dreamscapes. We traveled around this globe in the blink of an eye, yet still taking in all the wonder.

The globe was inhabited by every kind of animal you could think of; including man. We saw how man progressed on this tiny globe within this beautiful dreamscape.

Seth asked if we would like to take the time to experience evolution on a more physical level by slowing down our passage of time to that of the globes time stream then manifesting into a vessel that could mingle on this plain.

Bill wanted to watch as an observer so he remained as a photon. Before making this transformation we traveled much slower as photons ourselves. This would be a game of hide and seek for the children as they all agreed to take on forms in secrecy then look for each other on the globe. Mary and I would monitor the game to make sure that no one got really lost.

Mary and I took the form of our own physical bodies for this play. Penny became a teacher in a small village. Brandon became a minstrel traveling about. Charles was having so much fun as he closed off his vision so he could not see who and where everyone was hiding. He chose to hide as an alchemist living in the mountains overlooking the village that Penny was in. Charles chose the form of an older man but he could not mask his childlike playful mind. This would be so much fun for Charles.

Myra became a merchant that brought values to the people. She bartered with the inhabitants in a way that brought out all of their talents, producing goods that everyone could use.

Seth was the last to transform. He could be anything in this reality and he wanted to choose wisely. While traveling around the area of the game he saw this small little girl walking along the banks of a large stream. She danced and sang as she walked along. The little girl was known in the village as the shaman princess Shawna. The other children called her Grandmother Shawna because she was an old spirit in a child's body. You would not know that she was so advanced by just looking at her without truly seeing her. She played with the water; she picked up stones and placed them in her pouch. There was something special about Shawna that Seth did not discover right away.

Watching Shawna play gave Seth his inspiration on what to transform into for the game of hide and seek that they were playing. Seth became a small crystal rock about ten feet in front of Shawna's path. He placed himself in a spot that caught the sunlight just right so he would get Shawna's attention. He wanted Shawna to pick him for her pouch with her own free will.

At first Shawna walked right past Seth seeming not to have noticed this special rock at all. She then came running back, giggling as she picked Seth up saying; you thought I did not see you my sparkling little friend. You are going to be one of my favorite stones. When returning to her home Shawna placed all her stones on a shelf near her bed. She talked to all the stones so Seth was nothing but another one her loving collection. She would place each one of the stones in her own way asking questions and making statements to them like; you must have a wonderful story, you have been around for so long. She would ask the stones to tell her their stories.

Weeks would go by before Shawna would pick Seth of the shelf for some special attention. This was just a brief moment for Seth so it did not matter. Shawna gazed into the crystal Seth rock so Seth showed her sacred geometry by reflecting light on a nearby wall. Seth projected the seed of life, then the tree of life, then the flower of life.

Shawna reacted by saying; oh! You are going to be great fun, you are my teacher stone. Thank you precious one, please show me more.

Visions appeared in Shawna's mind that took her into Seth's world. Bit by bit she grasped concepts that many masters never realized on her small planet. She still did not know that she was a part of her pet rock's dreamscape.

One day there was a festival in the small village that people from all around would attend. Shawna would bring a whole pouch full of her favorite stones with her to the festival for trading. Everyone from the team playing hide and seek would be at this festival. Myra was there trading fine perfumes, spices, pottery and many other things. Charles was there trading gold, silver, iron and even transforming metals as a show for his trading. Penny had her classroom with her as she went from merchant to merchant. Her pupils followed her like a ducklings follows their mother. Brandon roamed the streets playing a fiddle, chanting lyrics of magical lore and adventures beyond the normal reality. Two of the most playful mice played with him as children

Shawna was drawn to the alchemist merchant display and she watch as he changed a lump of lead into a gold nugget. She asked the alchemist if he would trade the gold nugget for one of her stones. The alchemist looked at the stones and saw Seth among the other stones.

I'll take that one; the alchemist replied pointing at Seth.

Shawna quickly put Seth back in her pouch saying; you may have any of the others but I will keep that one. Look, this one has a wonderful story. He was formed in the deepest part of the planet and was pushed to the surface from a great eruption. The river moved him slowly to where he came to rest for hundreds of years in the spot where

I picked him from all the others. He told me his story and now I am telling you. Do you want to trade?

Can I hold the other stone; the alchemist asked?

Shawna felt trust so she pulled out her special stone and handed it to the alchemist. (Charles) the alchemist took the stone and held it close to his lips whispering in a joyful tone; I found you first.

Seth's mental laughter caused the stone to brighten then dim while Charles held it in his hand. Seth asked Charles to befriend Shawna to help her learn and Charles playfully agreed. He also agreed to not tell their secret to Shawna.

Charles handed the stone back to Shawna thanking her for sharing her rocks with him as he took the aged river stone that Shawna offered him for the gold nugget. I love this rock's story and I will give this rock many more stories to share. Charles also gave Shawna a gyroscope to play with and learn from.

Shawna would not take her Seth stone from her pouch for the rest of the festival.

Mary and I watched in the background keeping our thoughts clear so the players could not see us. We had such fun as they found each other. The festival also revealed Myra to Brandon. They teamed up to find the others. Penny would not be found for a while.

As Shawna grew older she began to resemble Seth's violet heart flame that he had lost early on in his life. She was taken in a car accident when Seth was only twenty two years old. Her spirit was alive in Shawna even if Shawna was not aware of it. Seth has always carried his first love with him his whole life and here she was manifesting all over again. Shawna's personality, her smile, her wit, her thirst for knowledge, her playfulness as well as her looks all remarkable resembled Seth's old girl friend Gloria.

Bill came to Seth one evening to let him know of some things that were happening on other parts of this small garden globe. Apparently Seth's memories of the dark cabals that used to exist on Earths had trickled into this world. One group on the planet was creating a currency that they insisted would make trade much easier for everyone. They would create this paper that represented a natural resource that people were using to make all their exchanges. This group of paper pushers or money makers was looking to take control of all the merchants with this new idea of a common means of exchange. This group made the money so they could charge everyone for the use of the paper money. The idea was spreading quickly.

Seth would have to show Shawna the consequences of this type of system becoming the normal mode of operation in any society. Shawna's influence on the people of that area was great, most everyone would listen to her.

At first Shawna did not understand the visions she was having while holding the Seth rock in her hand. She understood better when she went to the market place with her stones and many merchants wanted only the paper exchange instrument. This could lead to a system of control in a free will society she quickly noticed when comparing what was happening to her visions.

Shawna became an advocate for truly free trade without forced exchange instruments. She would talk to all the large gatherings including Penny's classroom. Shawna always had her pouch of stones with her when she went to speak with others. When questions were asked that she did not have the answer to Shawna would reach into her pouch and hold the Seth stone while answering.

Penny's classroom knew her as Miss Nickel. Miss Nickel introduced Grandmother Shawna (as she was known by this name) to the whole school to speak on one occasion. Shawna told the group about many things including some of the stories that were shared by the rocks and trees. When she came to the subject of the paper exchange concept that was taking over the trade, she reached into her pouch to hold the Seth stone in her hand.

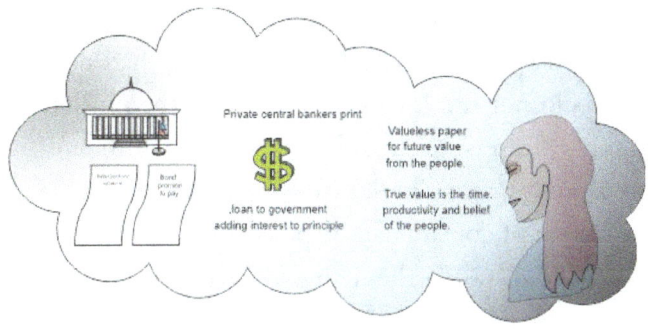

Shawna talked about concepts for society that she had never pondered. Spiritual Meritocracy planned resource evaluation and distribution, basic rights of all, abundance and scarcity, natural law, freedom along with the cost of freedom, self-determination and oneness. She channeled Seth thoughts with eloquence that kept the children in wonder.

The Seth stone glowed with a vibrant white light as she pulled it out of her pouch. Miss Nickel immediately noticed her old friend Seth and was thrilled that she found one of the team players in their game of hide and seek. Seth and Penny linked minds as he filled her in on what was happening. He could not let this group of money vipers loose on his garden paradise. They came from his memories so he had a responsibility to stop it from happening. Plus the game was still on and they still needed to find Myra and Brandon. He let Penny know that Charles was an alchemist that was already helping Shawna.

Now they could all help to bring about the awareness to the people about the consequences of the paper pushing society.

The school cheered as Grandmother Shawna finished speaking. She directed everyone to look inward for their answers and to use the data she was providing to help make informed decisions.

Meanwhile Bill had also contacted Myra and Brandon about what was going on. Myra was already feeling pressure as a merchant to switch over to this new paper paradigm. Brandon had a large pile of the paper that was being peddled on the people. Brandon had never lived in a monopoly society but he realized that the paper had no real intrinsic value. You could not use it to survive outside the illusion being sold. You could only clean yourself with it after a body function.

Penny, Brandon and Charles were seeing for the first time in their life how a system of control can be placed on a group of people. This appeared so unnatural to them that they instinctively knew that it was wrong.

The awareness of the intent of the paper pushers gained strength as songs were written and sung by everyone's favorite minstrel, Brandon. Brandon was calling himself The Brand Band and he was loved all over. Miss Nickel (Penny) already suspected that The Brand Band was Brandon so she invited Shawna to see the show that was being performed in the village square. Shawna was now twenty five of her years old. She had changed into a beautiful woman but she still held on to her child like mind, she loved to play.

After the show Miss Nickel urged Shawna to follow her to catch the Brand Band. Penny could not wait to tag Brandon as the game of hide and seek was coming to the conclusion. They had all found each other on this world. The stories were exchanged as Shawna watched on in awe.

Mary and I joined the group as they laughed about how clever they were. Shawna witnessed as they all returned to photons right in front of her. Seth took on the form of a man that Shawna was instinctively attracted to. He explained what was going on as best he could. It was hard for Shawna to comprehend that Seth was the creator source for all she knew and her existence. It also boggled her mind that the creator source she had been searching for was in turn seeking his creator source.

The team of photons stayed around as Seth and Shawna stopped the growth of the toxic money paradigm. Seth would spend the next thousand years married to Shawna. This was just a few moments in the dreamscape so we all waited for Seth to live his life with Shawna. What we did not expect was that Shawna would join us as photons for the rest of our dream vision vacation.

That evening of day two in our dream vacation was full of love as the story was shared with the rest of the dream voyagers. Scout and Jasmine loved the story the most.

We all agreed that we would all just relax on our third day here in our fifth dimensional dream reality. The third day would hold events that would bring relaxation but not the way we anticipated.

ALBERT'S JOURNAL OF THE UNIVERSE

3ʳᴰ ENTRY

COSMIC MOVIE

September 2nd-2045
Continued

On this third day Zeb came to visit bringing with him a crystal gem that held the records of a totally separate universe. This other universe is one of billions that exist in the Omni-verse. On one of our previous vision journeys we ventured into the Omni-verse to

witness the birth of our universe. Here we saw the mind boggling possibility of endless universes that make up the cells of still another larger Quasi-verse. This chain of existence is endless. Each universe including our own has a tourus energy field. Each universe came from source and was returning to source within an even larger energy field. This makes us all part of the GREAT I AM. This is my favorite name for the Omni-present. How do you name something this grand? Names create limits or boundaries, referring to a single existence. I believe that there is an even GREATER I AM and so on.

Everyone got comfortable as Zeb placed the crystal in the center of us, gathered in an open circle. I could not help but notice that the crystal looked a lot like the stone that Seth transformed into on our sojourn where we met Shawna. Crystals are used to store large amounts of knowledge; they are also used to archive galactic events.

Zeb gave us some opening thoughts before sharing the archive; "as you already know, things are not always the way we perceive them. How we perceive something has a great effect on any outcome. Perception is sometimes limited by knowledge or lack of knowledge. Reactions to our perceptions are guided by our basic emotions if we let that happen. We will explore two universes that have their own perspectives that react to the same potential event. We call this archive The Organic Omni-verse".

In front of us appeared a replica of the Omni-verse showing many multi-universes. The scene then focused on two neighboring universes one was just forming. The vastness between universes is hard to comprehend without observing this from a much larger vantage point. As we zoomed in 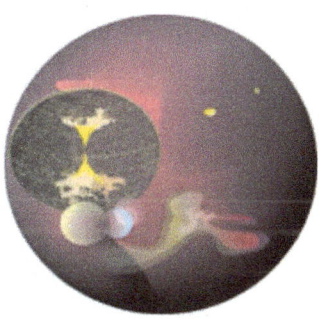 the distances became greater. The scene closed in on a large planet that was orbiting the outskirts of a universe. This would provide a unique vantage point for the planets inhabitants that observed the heavens. For one quarter of their cycle around their sun they saw the endless universe they were part of and for the second quarter of their orbit they saw what they termed as the upper horizon of their universe. For the third quarter of their orbit they saw only darkness they called the void. For the fourth quarter they saw the lower horizon of their universe. When facing the void they could not see even the light from any other universe because of the great distance and their size. If not for the reflections off the twin moons they would be in total darkness while facing the void.

The inhabitants of this remote planet called their home Paratara, which meant Perimeter Earth. They traveled through space on the skin or shell of their universe. Billons of their years passed without seeing any light coming from the void. As our other universe is birthed or comes into conception a new light appeared in the void for the first time ever. The Paritites had highly advanced technology so they sent a scout vessel out into the void to see what this new source of light was coming from. Because of the great distance of the void, it would take several of their years to hear back from the scout vessel.

The last message the Paritites received from the scout vessel only confirmed what their scientist suspected; this was another expanding universe heading right for them. Surely this would cause the destruction of both universes. Fear reached to their core. Each orbit of the planet showed a remarkable expansion of the approaching universe. Imamate doom was quickly approaching.

Many theories on how the destruction would take place circulated around Paratara. None of these theories had any positive outcomes. The Paritites reacted with hopelessness but also a determination to live the time they had left seeking happiness at any cost. Now they had the fear of total destruction to deal with but also a growing fear of each other.

Some of the Paritites felt a duty to worn the rest of their universe of the impending cosmic destruction so they sent out herald ships in every direction into their universe. The intention of this group of heralds was to show the facts to any inhabited worlds they came across. They were to do this without spreading fear. Many of the heralds were fearful themselves so the energy they brought with them would now reach many areas of their universe. They were spreading paralyzing fear throughout their known universe.

It took several more of the Paritites years before the original scout ship started to enter this new universe. They were well out of range for any communication. The scout ship had lost communication after their last report confirming the expanding universe that was heading towards their home world.

When they entered the new universe the first planet they came across that had what they considered intelligent life came on their sensors. The planet was known as Uroptimum.

This would be the scout vessels first contact and landing for this long journey they were on. The indigenes people of this world welcomed them with loving arms. These people also knew about the expanding universes coming collision, although they could not wait to encounter what they considered their cosmic sibling. The excitement of this coming event could be felt by the members of the Paritites scout ship. The energy was like a child has when they see their parents again after a separation. The longing to see these parents could also be felt; only the feeling of love was present.

The Paritites scout ship Captain showed the world all of their compounded data that pointed to the mutual destruction of both universes. Surely these Uroptimist must not have all the facts, knowledge or wisdom or they would be as fearful as the Paritites.

A delegate from the Uroptimist spoke up saying; everything consists of energy waves that have both a negative and a positive charge. The density or frequency of the waves cause illusions of mass as we photons travel through time/space. If we hold the frequency of love creation then no harm will come when our universes encounter each other. The same polarities of any magnetic field repel each other and it will be like a cosmic embrace as we come together. It is sad to find out that you have polarized yourself to the negative, this will only bring struggle along with unnecessary harm to your path back to source. You must return to your universe to spread this wisdom or our paths. As we embrace, it could be the most wonderful experience ever known by us. Otherwise it will not be a pleasant as it could be. We will approach you with only positive love vibrations. Our energies will not match with you in a fearful state of hopelessness.

The Paritites scout ship now had a new mission; take the long voyage back through the void, then spread the word in a fear filled universe that only love and acceptance will save them.

The scout vessel had no idea of the efforts of their home world to spread the fear far and wide into their known universe. The heralds that were sent out have visited many galaxies. Fear, survival, anger and all of the confused emotions that come along with fear was rippling through out their universe. The task ahead of the scout ship was going to be much harder than they could imagine. They would be almost forgotten when they get back as the voyage through the void had taken seventy five of their years to meet the Uroptimist. Three generations of their society will have come and gone. How many Paritites would be left with them in their fear filled state?

As things would have it the message that was spread by the Paritites heralds was not always welcome everywhere they traveled. Some of the worlds the heralds encountered that had intergalactic travel felt that they should just loot anything in their path as they traveled to the opposite end of the universe. This is where the destruction would not be felt by the colliding universes. These simple minded beings carved a path of chaos wherever they went. The galactic looters also spread the fear vibration where they went.

The Paritites were now responsible for the actions of these rouge species pillaging the universe. The world that held a better comprehension of source was now victims of this barbaric, egotist, parasitical beings that cared only for themselves. What a calamity of events; just because the Paritites had the wrong reactions to their perception of events that had not even occurred yet. The fear had caused a dis-ease in their universe.

The journey back through the void for the scout vessel only took them thirty six of their years as the universes were rapidly getting closer to each other. At the expansion rate of both universes they had about twenty years to change the beliefs of an entire universe. The scout ship's crew had to believe the message they brought back in order to convince others about the new perception of the approaching collision.

The crew did not get any welcome wagon when they returned. They had been within communication range for several years although they never got any real responses from their hails. They landed at what used to be the heart of activity for their globe with no one in sight. How could such an advanced society wither away in just a few generations?

The crew sends five of their members out to explore. This crew was now the children of the original crew. They had spent most of their lives traveling through the void with only shared images of the home planet that their parents knew. This was nothing like those projected images. However; they grew up without the fear that had taken root. Their parents only shared the love that they felt with the Uroptimist.

A crowd soon gathered around the five dispatched crew members. They were truly different than anyone else. They had an aura of confidence without the arrogance of ego. They had a glow of energy that attracted their polar opposite that the people were used to feeling. Somehow the negativity had no effect on them, it rolled off of them because they brought back with them another frequency that was now being remembered by those that they have contact with. This was no miracle transformation that the people had; one had to open themselves up for the memories of fearlessness to resurface within each individual.

One of the Paritites stepped out from the crowd asking; "who are these visitors, where did they come from"?

They were surprised that the response was in their own language and did not need a translating devise.

The eldest from the crew answered; "I am called Jarod, we are the sons and daughters of the scout ship your ancestors sent into the void over a hundred and eleven years ago. We have been to the beyond and returned. We bring back a message of love and hope".

The man from the crown; "I am Esop from the clan Hypicrus and those you see before you are now the humble servants of the global cabal that calls themselves the Litest. While everyone was governed by fear they found their opportunity to take control by claiming hidden knowledge that offered hope.

They have kept the fear alive with their minions along with the technological advantages they have. How do we know if you are not of the same intention"?

Jarod laughed to himself saying; "we are not here to govern anyone, you must govern yourself. That is the only way to get your answers. Your so called forced obedience is purely an illusion. These so called **Litest** have served the purpose of bringing an as-semblance of order where only chaos was around. They may have perpetrated the chaos to begin with. That is why you must not seek them for answers. Their purpose is ended if you govern yourself. You must do this change yourself. We cannot do anything for you but show you the new perspective of our shared existence".

"We have a big task ahead of us sharing this new perspective that is actually older than anyone can imagine. This perspective of unconditional love is what will bring order back out of the chaos that your fears have caused you and infected this universe. There are cosmic forces at hand coming from source that insure that if you are in line with source or unconditional love then no harm will come to your immortal spirit, you will learn from your experience".

"First you have to change yourself, and then you can change our home planet Paratara and then work on the harm that was caused in the universe. We cannot do this for you so do not look to us for answers. We will help you if you allow this, or you can help us fulfill our mission past down from our parents. We are here to open up a new perspective that will bring salvation by sharing what our parents gave us (love)".

Esop busted out in frustration; "you have no idea just what has taken place over the last one hundred years. Paratara now has three ruling cities that hold the resources of the entire planet. One city controls the religious beliefs of our planet and claim dominion on the land or vessel our spirits reside in. The second city controls the instruments of commerce; they have inserted micro-chips in everyone that track everything we do. If they are not pleased with our conformity they simple turn off your chip. This started out with the chips in identification cards then coerced the populous to except the injection of the chips. The third city controls the military of our home planet, this city controls all travel, communication, technology and determines who lives or is exterminated".

"It does not stop here; they have spread fear throughout the universe causing whole planets to be ecologically raped by marauders that the three cities secretly support. The **Litest** are looking to spread their control to a galactic level as the same course of events that happened here are now happening on many other worlds".

"The enforcers for the **Litest** are either fixated with their illusion of status or thriving in their illusion of power. They have a much better living standard than the rest of us, that is maintained to insure our loyalty. Some of these enforcers are just not capable of seeing the big picture so they only do what they are told by the great computer. Some of the enforcers take great pleasure in the illusion of power granted to them as they arrogantly push the regulations of the three cities in all situations. These are the ones that move up in their ranks to a higher standing with the **Litest**. Most of the lower ranking enforcers think they are 'doing good' by following the protocols of an ordered system. They do not even consider that there is another much better way to exist".

"These three cities work together to maintain and spread the system of control they have outlined and orchestrated so well".

Jarod; "you paint a very grim picture my friend Esop. What you are **not** seeing is that all of what you are saying was done with your consent. Maybe you consented because of a lack of knowledge or under duress but you consented anyway. With new knowledge you can withdraw your consent. This may be difficult at first; giving up your learned behavior then withdrawing your consent. It will come naturally as you look within guided by love".

"Love is a force within that is more powerful than fear. Once you tap that force, fear begins to fade. Your fears will not give in easily as they keep blocking your path. The vibrations of love will sooth the fears so you can overcome them to move on. Soon the vibration will become like a wave that washes the fears away. Your polarity will change so that our two universes can embraces, making an exchange of energy that will enhance all existence. This wave starts with each of you. Start the wave detached to any results that may happen. Do not confront or be at odds with your current situation, instead create on your own what you find in your heart center. Do not dwell on the way you believe things to be".

The wave that started that day did spread like wild fire. The inhabitants of Paratara started creating ways to live outside the system of control. They stopped giving their energy and withdrew their consent to anything that was not centered in love. Private agendas that were not in center were easily exposed and support stopped for these agendas. What took the alleged **Elite** over a century to put into place was being unraveled in just a couple decades.

As the archive that Zeb was sharing ended the two universes seemed like they were dancing with each other as they merged. A **Vessica Pisces** was formed that would link the dancing universe together creating a marvel within the Omni-verse that would be duplicated over and over throughout the GREAT I AM.

The sharing from Zeb took up with we conceived as our day on our dream vacation so we all set off to rest. It was interesting to see events unfold in other realities that seemed to mirror the events that took place on our own planet Earth.

ALBERT'S JOURNAL OF THE UNIVERSE

4ᵀᴴ ENTRY

SOURCE WHISPERER

September 2nd-2045
Continued

Nothing prepared us for the dynamic encounter that we would all have the next day cycle of our dream vacation. We had no real plans for our activities for the day. Our itinerary had not been planned; our intentions were not even being discussed. Everyone was content with just being in the moment. Thoughts, questions, poseurs', concepts, theories, calculations and all left brain logical thinking was temporarily shut down.

As usual it will be very difficult to place words or descriptions on the experience we were having. All sound was one sound vibrating complete, all vibrations were interconnected like a cosmic/divine tapestry. Our dream vacation reality was engulfed with a spiraling energy field. We became part of the fabric within the tapestry, (we realized our connection would be a more accurate statement). The density of our dream reality seemed to compress to form mass in yet another plain of existence. We found ourselves going through an even larger vortex that gently placed us on a world where we were but a speck. We entered a living being on this world as a compressed photon or hard light.

The being that we entered seemed to have very little of what we consider brain activity. The senses of this being were very strong and it just reacted to outside stimulus in an instinctual manner, no emotions were attached to any reaction it had. We were like a spark of consciousness that awakened a part of this being, long dormant or possible totally unfamiliar to this reality. As a group photon we managed to keep our chattering logical brain quite as we assimilated the surroundings we were in. Mary was very helpful in keeping the chatter to a minimum. As we accustomed ourselves, our host being was approached by another being that was attempting to harness the being we were now one with. Our host first instinct was one of fight or flight although our presence caused a different reaction as our host being stood still, gazing at this new opposing force.

These beings now approached each other with caution as the one seeking to take control was now reaching out to our host in gestures of friendship. We could hear the words' being spoken from our host's advisory as he approached. Brandon helped comprehend the language that was being spoken.

The intent of entrapment or forced submittal to another's wills was no longer part of the encounter that these beings were having. Instead a bond of friendship was being sparked as the two of them came closer. It was then that we became aware of some of our host attributes as she/we spread our enormous wings while standing up on our hind legs. What kind of being are we. Most of us wondered? We quickly silenced our chattering questions so we could just experience our unfolding story. We had already caused change within our host although it was purely unintentional. This simple change would have astounding effects in this world we were visiting. Seth's experience as a shape shifter has helped us all in our capacity to become something without it becoming us.

Without the intent of entrapment a trust was silently created. This new trust had no master/servant relationship. The trust created a bond between these two beings that would mutually benefit both beings. This was a magical moment for this reality as both beings changed their perceptions of each other, to create a relationship with each other that was well out of the conceptions of the others inhabiting this world.

As our host became friends with his old advisory they started to travel together. When we got to a large lake with smooth surface we got to see what our host looked like for the first time in this experience. He/she/we are huge in comparison to our new friend. We could easily overcome any advances that were not in services to both with harmful intent. Our host chose to allow his new friend to ride on our back so we could cover more ground. Our new friend or trustee of our mutual trust has agreed to maintain our trust with unconditional love. He calls himself At-land and calls our host Unis.

Part of our trust with Unis is to make sure no harm comes from anything we may do or think. Unis has taken on several new trust agreements as we have seen so far traveling with her. Our presence is barely known to her but a trust had to be formed before we could enter. Her new trust with At-land would not happen with many of At-lands brethren. She/we could sense the ridicule that At-land had to take for not beating Unis into submitting to his will.

Unis took notice of how her fellow species was enslaved and treated badly by the others of At-lands kind. She did this on her own without our help or influence, although we had some small impact on how she was reacting.

At-land was known by his peers as a great sorcerer or one in touch with source. Those that ridiculed At-land did their slander behind his back. He would just laugh at their pettiness if he heard any of it. His laughter would reverberate loudly with a genuine tone of amusement. Rumors were around that At-land had bewitched Unis into compliance and did not need a whip.

A simple act of kindness can be construed in some very strange ways if they are not in line with what you believe. Both Unis and At-land were the first of their kind to be something different, to act from inner guidance, this was perceived as magical to the blocked mind or from a lower perspective.

Unis saw how it was her kind that was creating everything. At-land's fellow beings the Organites used her species the Conformites for most of the labor that went into doing anything. Some of the Conformites even fly as war creatures in battles among the Organites. We could feel confusion within Unis as she asked herself; how could we let this happen? We could also feel how Unis missed her old ways when she was not aware of all the injustice and primitive behavior. She missed the ignorance of not knowing. That ignorance is how it all came about; so Unis was determined to make some changes.

The Organites treated the Conformites like a commodity that they traded. The bargaining chip was the Comformites willingness to comply with your wants and needs. Unis was not worth much in their illusionary currency system.

Unis was perplexed at how to proceed with her new intent. Most of her kind was satisfied with their lives as slaves. Some of them even had really nice comfortable pens to lock themselves in at night. All of her kinds were missing the spark that she had that day she met At-land. Unis communicated with her fellow Conformites how they were much larger in stature than the Oganites and greater in numbers. She communicated about her trust agreement with At-land and how it was mutually considerate of each other. She quickly got a reputation of being a rebel so she was avoided by many. Her intent was getting harder to accomplish the harder she worked at it.

One day Unis spread her mighty wings and took us on a journey with At-land on her back. Unis communicated with At-land freely now; telling him about her experiences. We flew over the most breathtaking scenery one could only imagine. Not even in our dream scape did we come close to some of the wonders and abundance on this world?

Our soul group that was part of Unis still had a trust agreement of non- interference, although we could feel her wave of emotions as she pondered her freedom. Memories of the times when she roamed without a care in the world returned to her. It was her touch back with nature that would be the answer to her problems fulfilling her intent to bring awareness to her fellow Conformites.

At-land explained to Unis that she was now listening to the source whisperer that is inside all beings. He told Unis that he was listening to his source whisperer on the day they met and he has been following that inner guidance ever since. Their friendship was a gift from source that is worth more than all the treasures anywhere. Our trust and our bond is the most valuable thing in existence. They know that what we have come together to form is greater than any of their previous agreements although they are afraid of change. Just because they do not believe something does not take the truth away. You must allow others the opportunities to find out things on their own. Make a gesture or comment facing them in an alternative path, then let them alone. Soon they will come to you with all of these revelations that inspire them.

Unis was refreshed when she returned from her natures (fly about) with At- land. She had a new resolve to become detached from achieving any results, just to act from inner guidance. She would only take advice from her source whisperer.

Our soul group had to be extra careful now not to influence Unis in her free will decision making. We do not want to be mistaken as a higher source! Maybe we had already interfered too much but we all believe that what happened in our first encounter was meant to happen.

At times, Mary had her task full keeping the soul group quite, about to strain itself. Each of us would react a different way and it is hard watching others stumble about if you can help. We all had advice for Unis but we could not voice our advice without breaking our trust agreement of non-interference. If she knew we were part of her and asked for our advice then as long as we are not recognized as a higher authority we can answer. The problem is we cannot spark the knowledge of our presence without breaking the trust.

As Unis was now aware of who she was and her connection to source she attracted to her many that had the same awareness to them. This idea of freedom needed to be remembered. Trust had to be re-established. We all need to be free to use our energy where we chose. The Consentites had to change their name also. They would no longer be referred to as Consentites. Now with this new wave of consciousness; they were to be called the Non-concentites. Bless you!

Things would not change easily as the Organites did not want to give up their illusion of control. Working in trust and creating bonds was a way of control not meant to benefit anyone but the Organites. Unis noticed that the Organite's have also unknowingly enslaved themselves in their battle for control. They were slaves to their beliefs and their egos. Nothing could get accomplished without the help of one of the Consentites yet the Organite's held their illusion of control.

At-land was now being perceived as a threat by his fellow Organites as he introduced unparalleled ideas that were not in compliance to structured society. The self-appointed authorities went to the make believe leaders to petition the capture of At-land to silence him forever. Just his unusual relationship with Unis was enough to prosecute At-land for non-compliance.

However, At-land was true to his name sake; drawing his energy from the universe around him, he stood on his ground with many others that supported their right to think and act freely as long as no harm is committed. The Organites argued that At-land was bringing harm to society; if they lost control of the labor force that brings comfort to all Organites.

Unis was being held with At-land in a quarantined area where they could not even talk to each other. We could all feel her despair as she searched inside for answers. Her thoughts went to the first meeting where she felt that spark that caused her to react so differently towards At-land that day.

Our soul group was surprised that Unis had taken notice of us; we were nothing but an impulse, photon or neutron. Although we were aware of our initial impact we have been very successful at keeping our presence unknown ever since. She referred to us as Spark.

"I felt you enter me that day; Spark. You were no more than a flash of awareness but I felt you and allowed your entry with an open heart. I am not sure why you are here or why I haven't heard from you since that day. I know that you are still with me Spark. I feel that you are looking for answers also. Maybe we can renew our trust to include a mutual exchange for all. I am asking for your help"!

Our soul group emerged from Unis like a pin sized point of light that quicky became larger. Our light sphere then opened up for us all to show ourselves as individuals to Unis. We were all so excited, Scout, Jasmine, Charles, Brandon and Penny were bursting with energy waiting to be unleashed. Mary had to help them release that energy in a constructive manner; one at a time they gave their input on how we could help.

Unis was surprised at what was unfolding in front of her. She saw us leave her heart center as a photon of light, split into many photons then take shapes of who we are. This is a lot to except from anyone's imagination. Alone in the solidarity of her confinement she was going crazy. Myra (as a healer) stepped up to Unis to help settle her disease. Mary also helped in explaining who we were along with our intent. Brandon made sure that everyone could communicate with no miss-comprehensions.

I was amazed at how we all played our rules in this unfolding or disclosure. We were now able to share the wisdom we were acquiring with a world that needed a spark if insight. The first thing we did was to re-establish the communication between At-land and Unis. At-land understood our connection with source. As a sorcerer he traveled many cosmic pathways and has met guides from many realities. He welcomed us with open arms. Al-land also accepted us because we looked a lot like the Organites when we assumed our physical shape.

Still the question of how to enact change in a free will society with unwillingness to change was confronting us. Most all would recognize the benefit of a more heart centered existence if they could only tap into the memories they had before their learned behavior set in. How do we get them to tap these memories?

At-land insisted that Unis and his trail be made public. His captors did not want a public hearing in fear of releasing new thoughts to the population. Both At-land and Unis had friends that helped spread the opinion of having an open forum for all to listen. Crowds gathered around the hearing chamber questioning the assumed authority of the captors and petitioning the release of both At-land and Unis.

First the bloodthirsty captors brought At-land out in chains in front of the crowd. A well versed speaker spoke to the gathering masses. His rhetoric was well known as public opinion so he did not expect much resistance.

"I am Propagandious from the high council; we bring before you this trader At-land who wishes to stop our world as we know it and allow for equality between two sets of beings, where one is obviously meant to be of service to us. This has how it has been for thousands of years and it is still true today. The Consentites may be larger than us with abilities we cannot match but we have a psychological advantage with our technology and our ability to create, to reason. We are a step up in evolution and everything is here to serve us, including the Consentites. It is our destiny to rule. It is your destiny to rule. We must keep our agendas clear, without the muddled ideas of a quack conjurer and his rebel Consentite Unis".

With these words they brought Unis out, also in chains. It was obvious that Unis had been beaten. Our soul group felt the beatings that the Organites gave Unis before this public display. Many of us had never experienced this kind of derogating treatment so Mary and Myra helped healing the emotional wounds that got inflicted on us as well as Unis.

Propagandious went on saying; "look at this pathetic creature that At-land risk his life for. Even with her grand stature we have made her succumb into our servitude. We are truly the masters of our environment. Her memory of this beating will insure us of a lifetime of loyalty. If we coddle to her she would plan even more chaos. We are protecting you from that chaos".

All on her own (without the help or advice from our soul group) Unis stood up proudly saying; "I have only one higher authority. That authority is my own personal Source whisperer. This Source whisperer is shared with all existence so it is within everyone here. This includes my dear captor Propagandious who has taught me that I am not this physical body. We are all so much more than what we believe we are. We are all part of one shared dream that can be shaped any way we chose. Thank you Propagandious for your lesson but you did not teach me what you intended to teach me. No matter what you do you cannot make yourself an authority over others unless they allow this. You do not have my consent or my fear, or my compliance to your primitive mindset".

We could feel Unis drawing energy from the universe within her as she spoke. Her love for Propagandious was genuine and the crowd picked this up. We noticed a feeling of bewilderment as the crowd realized that Unis had forever turned the tables on the Organites by showing the Organites primitive behavior, therefore balancing the illusionary status of either race.

There was no need for a violent uprising as Unis's act of love brought along a new perspective. Both At-land and Unis were released as Propagandious found his way safely away from the turning tides of change that did not hold him in favor.

Our soul group vacationers all felt we were done here; our experiences had a new twist to them, learning to be detached from experience that someone you have come to love as part of you is finding their own path. We all have our own source whisperer and it whispers hints on our journey back to source. The GREAT I AM.

Unis followed us into the night sky embracing out light as we made our departure.

What was in store for us the next day of our vacation dream multi-universe was just as marvelous or enlightening as any experience we had so far. At this point we all went through the rest cycle of our vacation.

ALBERT'S JOURNAL OF THE UNIVERSE

5ᵀᴴ ENTRY

SOUND VIBRATIONS

September 2nd-2045
Continued

When we looked at the recordings of the lab after our shared dream vacation we saw that many of the beings we came connected to within the dream scape had returned with us as photons. The dreamscape would always be there for us to visit or we could simply create another. I am getting ahead of myself as I write this journal, although there is a purpose for bringing up the lab's camera recordings before we proceed with the journal. For now, let's back up to where we left off by telling about Brandon's experience within his dream visions.

After our rest, we all gathered once again to journey together. Brandon's ability to communicate with all species, beings, life, nature and all vibrational language has helped us in all the journeys that we have been experiencing.

Brandon's personal challenge was to find a dialect he could not understand or comprehend. This quest would lead us to a dark realm that Brandon, Charles and Penny had yet to experience in their current incarnation as our children. The levels of communications within our group had no barriers. We knew about Brandon's challenging quest without any spoken words. We were all playfully acceptant to accompany Brandon.

Our children were star beings that have been experiencing source spirit for thousands of re-incarnations so our new journey takes us back to Brandon as he was in another life cycle. In this incarnation Brandon was a Lawyer for the Crown during the inquisition. We immediately felt a strong dis connection with anything other than the physical reality that his previous lifetime was living through. An air of arrogance permeated the energy field that this being portrayed; Brandon could hardly believe that he perceived existence in this limited egotistical manner at any time within his journey into our shared reality, even in a previous life. We observed his past incarnation with the same interest Brandon had. We reminded Brandon to observe without judgment. His quest had led us here and we were determined to find the un-comprehension-al language. Why were we here?

Brandon was the most perplexed with this question. This was a vision based on his previous life and his memories of being here were as fresh as if he was reliving it all over. He knew that language was subject to individual interpretation and learned definitions and in this previous life he had used that knowledge to change the meanings of words to benefit himself as an imagined superior being. Even the remembered experience of love in this incarnation brought un-easy feelings of regret, yet Brandon remained non- judgmental and detached. It seems that Brandon's mastery of language came with some hard lessons that would eventually develop into this divine spirit we call Brandon.

Sir James Beth Aragon was his old incarnation. Lord Aragon was very influential with the Kings that were making claims of dominion, churches that had agenda's and the pawns that served the self-created leaders. He played a deadly game of deceit in the chess board reality he believed himself to be in. Programming the populous into accepting his shared perceptions of status conflicts, getting others to except his delusions of authority was achieved by his fluent rhetoric. He smiled quietly to himself as others assimilated their energy towards his barbaric paradigm. He was quick to shun or persecute those who saw reality differently. Lord Aragon's language was being guided by a limited selfish intent along with a narrow perspective. For Lord Aragon words were like daggers of persuasion yet as intelligent as he believed himself to be he failed to reach beyond the physical realm. He saw the value in how the churches controlled the beliefs of the masses by only sharing half-truth mixed in with illusion. He kept the knowledge of everyone's divine connection with source a secret from others as if he was the only one who knew.

Lord Aragon lived in London where the Christian Church was accepted by most of the populace. Those who held on to ancient wisdom were prosecuted for their beliefs or wisdom. Many of the great minds of his time were burned as witches or demons after a mockery of a trial. Lord Aragon was responsible for many of these death sentences. He knew that critical thinking was more dangerous that whole armies; so opposing perspectives to him or the church had to be silenced quickly. One of his opposing forces was the maiden Osiris who was full of love.

The maiden Osiris shared healing freely. She had ancient knowledge taught to her by her grandfather who was a Druid sorcerer. Her natural way of bringing joy to those around her made her an attraction amongst the people. The King at this time period was placing himself at the right hand of what he called God, this was placing himself above the church who already had an illusionary claim to that position. People were being forced, coerced, bribed or put to death for not complying with the Kings fantasy. The maiden Osiris knew that nothing stood between us and our creator so she was risking her life for her knowingness. She also knew that anything that is forced on you against your will is not your will.

When our team of dream journeyers came across maiden Osiris she was instantly recognized as a past re-incarnation of Penny. All of the memories of this past life returned to Penny as soon as she made contact with the maiden Osiris. We all felt her shock as she realized that her dear brother Brandon was once her nemesis.

Maiden Osiris shared what many felt was common knowledge with her closest family and friends. Her words put everything into a harmonious perspective that rang true to those who searched for truth. Unfortunately her words did not fit the agendas of the King and Lord Aragon. Her outspoken way was tolerated until maiden Osiris made a statement that she quoted from the bible that the church stood behind; "I am" the lord thy God, Though shalt have no false gods before me. By placing the king or the church between you and God you are breaking their first commandment. This commandment tells you that you are God (I am). Each of us is God along with everything we see, hear, smell, touch or experience.

By making this statement of truth the Maiden was marked by the monarch, leading to a search and capture order from the king. She could be put to death for not accepting the Kings status. What the king failed to recognize was that all men and women are KINGS and QUEENS. His status was the illusion that gave him authority over those that consented or validated his claim.

The perils maiden Osiris was subjected to grow as we all felt Penny's uneasiness remembering these events. She wanted to worn her previous self of the coming events although there was a healing going on within her that she did not quite comprehend. We proceeded viewing the events that unfolded without judgment or attachment. Many versions of this same story have already occurred in many dimensions so why should we create another.

As fate would have it the maiden Osiris was finally caught, then brought before Lord Aragon for trial and retribution. Lord Aragon immediately questioned the maiden by twisting her words. He asked her if she stood behind her claim to be God and greater than the king or church?

The maiden replied by saying; "I am neither above nor below anything; we are all part of prime creation". "Does a bird claim to be a bird"? "Making claims on things is a learned behavior. If you claim you are something or own something you are only creating an illusion".

"And yet you make statements attesting to your claims of grandeur"; Aragon snaps back. "Many have heard your claims and hold witness to your treason to the church and Crown". "You will be held accountable for your outspoken acts against the STATE."

Osiris spoke with certainty; "My intent was to show others they held the source within and they should not give that away". "If my words hold truth then that is for others to determine". "You cannot extinguish or crush an idea. Thoughts exist for all to hear even if they are not spoken in words." "All one has to do is be willing to listen to their inner wisdom".

Aragon rationalized his thoughts before speaking again. He knew that what Osiris was saying was true truth although it was not serving the agendas of the Crown. This common sense wisdom could spread like a dis-ease foiling all the illusions that have been so carefully and methodically put in place. How would the sheep survive without control? They need us to lead them, they ask us to lead them.

After a pause Aragon sternly turns towards Osiris saying; "what you are saying will only cause anarchy then chaos. The sheeple need guidance to build a society that will survive. They need protection from the terrible forces that can so easily subdue them into a fate far worse than what we offer".

Brandon was astonished at his (Aragon's) psychotic rational. Maybe this was the un-comprehentional language he was searching for. Here was a language of manipulation. If there is no demon to cause fear then create one. We all continued observing without judgment.

Osiris was not given the opportunity to reply as Aragon ushered for the guards to take her to the dungeons until the death ceremony. She is held for two years so most would forget the words of truth that she voiced, and then she was re-introduced to the populace as the hieratic traitor that was condemned for causing public unrest.

Aragon fine-tuned his rhetoric by re-defining common words used by the people. He gave new meaning to words then taught these new meanings to those that held him as an authority. This would be a language that could condemn anyone that is not familiar with his interpretation. He called these hidden word meanings (the language of law) to give them illusionary substance. This was also a language of jesters or outburst of emotions such as indignity or righteousness. Slamming your fist on a table to create a diversion was one of these tactics. It is not always what is said but what is allowed to be heard. Once one consented to play his game they already lost the game.

Aragon realized that getting validation was more powerful or profitable than teaching the true wisdom. If the majority believe in a lie then that make it the truth. This was Aragon's secret philosophy so he diverted his full attention seeking approval or validity for his twisted agenda. Weave the truth in with the lie so that it is harder to find and much more believable. [De]-noun-ce, [de]-feat, [de]-fraud, [de]-ceive and [de]-value are weapons of subversion or aids in validation. All of these tactics were used before the final death ceremony for Osiris.

On the day of final reckoning for Osiris where she would return to prime creator with open arms a new player came into the game. Aragon was at his best in manipulating the crowds, there to make witness for the event. Osiris was brought out before everyone in a state of weakness, malnutrition and dehydration. She was tied to a cross to be burned.

As Aragon announced the alleged crimes against the Crown, Church, State, and common welfare of the people, the Court Jester made a dynamic entrance with a handful of sparkling fireworks. Doing acrobatics while dancing and laughing; he quickly out shined Aragon and his boring rhetoric.

The bells on the jesters head seamed to play a tune as he finally spoke; "what a wonderful occasion we are all attending". "I expect to see smiles on every face, laughter coming from your spirits and love in your heart as we put to death this vile creature of divine origin". "Come and laugh with me to celebrate the demise of a free thinking being in a corporal vessel". "How wonderful it is to deny something that is out of the ordinary". "Believe what they tell you for it is what they want you to believe; after all they are your protectors". As he took out his play fishing pole to further play with the crowd he could see armed guards quickly surrounding him. With a series of hand springs he made his way to the cross of Osiris.

The guards approached looking as menacing as could be. They meant business that was sure. Picking up a torch then lighting it he playfully smiled saying; "wait a minute men", "I am on your side". "Here, I will set her on fire for you". "You can watch while you are grateful that it is not your spouse or siblings getting burned to death". "Smile, be happy, don't be such grumpy people on this happy day".

Not quite sure what to do the guards looked to Aragon for a sign. Aragon responded with a clenched fist telling them to snatch the jester. The crowd was in chaos as this all took place and many of the spectators stepped between the guards and the jester as he continued his playful rambling.

In a loud, boisterous, comical voice he approached Osiris with his lit torch saying; "you have been a naughty girl, haven't you"? "You spoke about love and self- worth"! "Come on, admit it". "You placed yourself along-side the crown and not beneath it". "How dreadfully insane you must be".

"I will burn you for this treachery, you unholy demon spawn". "Only our glorious protectors can determine what we think".

With that he turns to the gathering, an even larger amount of spectators than before. Most were confused but there was an air of levity. Some confusion arose in the crowd. It was a mixture of anger, laughter and self-realization although most listened intently.

The jester started out with a bow to the crowd; "I would like a volunteer from the audience!" "Someone that is capable of critical thinking". "Come on"! "There must be some thoughtful people out there." "You, good sir! Did I see you raise your hand?" "Do you think you are capable of independent thought?" "Yes?" "Guards, grab him!" "We are all going to have a party today" "A double burning."

"Can you feel the excitement building?" "Anyone else like to volunteer?" "Wait, I see that some of you would like to see me burn to death as well." "That just might happen, don't leave until the show is over." "Wow, A triple burning, what a story to tell your friends and family." "Ya Bubba, you should have been there." "The guards grabbed this babbling jester with a funny hat and burned him as well." "The screams were all different from each one." "What a spectacle"!

Charles was the first to notice, he turned to me and said; "that is me, daddy, I remember this. This is not a happy ending."

We all felt Charles as he recalled the climax of this life time's drama. Charles turns to Brandon and says; "next time I want to play the bad guy." "Do we have to watch this part?" "Osiris sounded like a golden siren, the volunteer was baritone and I laughed to the end."

"I do not want to see or experience this again"; Brandon spoke up. "I had nightmares about this and now I know the story behind those dreams". "The people were shaking in their boots after that." "It wasn't until I returned to source that I realized my greedy purpose in that life."

"I was not sure until now but the volunteer was me in that time period"; Bill admitted. "I remember looking out at thousands of people with their own set of eyes, observing the events from all different perspectives." "I remember feeling all the mixed emotions that were being generated as the jester worked the crowd." "We all started to laugh when he told the guards to grab me." "I was surprised when they did grab me to burn with you." "Charles, what you did as a court jester in that gathering had a lasting effect on most all, proving that you cannot kill a thought."

"The language of deceit with the intent of greedy manipulation is a language I once spoke but could no longer comprehend"; Brandon said in levity. "We get our answers in ways we least expect sometimes."

That finished another day of our shared dream vacation so I will be wrapping up on this journal entry. This was an enlightening day, full of surprises. We all share these life journeys and it is sometimes a small universe where we keep bumping into each other to help us along or pull us back. Sometimes we learn from our mis-takes but forget how the lesson was learned. Brandon glimpsed his dark-side in a previous life and it was a remembering that he needed to experience again. I am sure we all face that challenge when it presents itself to us.

ALBERT'S JOURNAL OF THE UNIVERSE

6TH ENTRY

CONCEPTUAL LOSS

September 2nd-2045
Continued

What happened the next day could be a paradox that we may never forget yet this day in our dream vacation was all about forgetting. I am not even sure how I will be able to relate this story or even how I am writing this journal.

We all woke up from our dream sleep feeling wonderful although we had no word thoughts or recognition of our relationships with each other. We gathered around one another as kindred spirits. All our  names, statuses, language, knowledge, behavior patterns and virtually everything we think we know was wiped from our minds.

We smelled each other, looked each other over with caution even got familiar in a playful manner as sibling puppies may do when first discovering one another. Everything was new as we explored our surroundings instinctually marking our territory or way back or whatever. We were there to play.

We were like new born children but without any parents or guiding force to teach us how to interpret what we experienced. We were in action/re- action mode (so to speak). The only way I am able to write this is because when the day or should I say lifetime ended our prefabricated memories that we believe make us who we are, returned to us. Only by sharing stories am I able to give this account for this magical day.

Our group of dream vacationers remained with the dreamscape we created at the beginning of our vacation. Everything we needed was still there for us although all of it was new or unfamiliar to us.

We have lived out many lifetimes on this dream vacation where we acted as observers or even participants to the stories that unfolded. Living an entire lifetime in one day that is really only a couple hours in our corporal starting point where we are recording our physical bodies and environment while we are on this shared dream vacation. There are many surprises in recordings that I have alluded to in previous entries. That will have to wait because at this point in our vacation it is not relevant.

This lifetime started out with a blank slate. As we encountered things for the first time they had no names attached to them. We did not know the words to make descriptions or place a name. We explored everything with a fresh set of senses and feelings. If something smelled good, we either licked it, poked it, played with it, ran around it or we ate it. We tested the limits of what we could do without fear, only curiosity. There was no concept of individuality. Without seeing our reflection back from a mirror or calm pool of water, we saw the surrounding dream scape and each other but not ourselves.

Cycles of brightness and dim progressed in front of us (days and nights) creating certain urges within us. We watched each other grow in size causing changes in our appearances to one another. It is amazing that even in this completely open/blank mind that my dear Mary and I still found each other as partners. The others saw what we had found with each other causing a reunion with a different status matrix than the ones we known before.

It seems that the mice and children had a much better grasp as to adapting, learning and thriving. Even though we did not identify them as the mice and children until the dream day/lifetime was complete. We also found out that we were spending the day with Scout and his tribe of mice on this amazing dream vacation, as mice. We all started out as a large litter of newborn mice. The playing field was leveled all the way across the board. Even Scout and his tribe started out as infants along with us. Here we were; this large litter of baby mice with no adult figures or guides along our path. If we had any concept of fear then that would have scared us to death.

All we saw and experienced was wonder. Wonder without thoughts of wonder. There was danger around us but with no concept of danger we moved about freely until danger or something new came across out path. We had created this dream scape with our full memory data banks so it had everything the physical world had. Rivers, mountains, trees, animals, sky, beaches, ocean even buildings and technology were still there although it was all being discovered for the first time by us.

For the first few weeks of out infant life as mice things were rather uneventful. Somehow our basic needs were provided. I believe that some of the mice tribe choose to be caretakers during this period, but they were not there when we opened our eyes and started moving around for the first time. Even then there was always food and water for our litter to consume. As we grew we had to become independent of this mystery nutrition source as it seemed to dwindle away. This caused us to expand our realm of awareness. Scout naturally took on his role of explorer and I would often join him on his foraging missions.

It is quite miraculous that our life essences developed in a new way as we grew into children. We no longer had the gifts of thought consciousness or the ability to communicate in any type of spoken dialect however we seemed to instinctively work with each other knowing what each of us could do to help us all out. I guess it can be compared to a physical body; the heart does not tell the hands to move and the hands do not control the heart but somehow both do their job to help out the whole body. When one part of the body is in discomfort the rest of the body takes action to aid or comfort by meeting the needs of that ailing member of the whole. This is how our tribe worked without us even being aware of this.

Bill would also accompany Scout and I on many foraging missions although he ran around every new encounter, examining it from every angle. He would spend time just running around something we came across, he would touch it, smell it, climb on it, look at it closely then back off to see it from a distance. It was like he was gathering data but there were no real thought patterns going on. His recall is that he was just extremely curious.

We were always extra cautious when we came across anything that moved around as we did. As I noted before our environment was the dreams scape we set up when we started our dream vacation. On one of our first gathering missions we came across Purr-puss the cat only we did not know her anymore. She was just a new obstacle to our mission. Scout spotted her from a distance then quickly ushered us behind a boulder so we would not be noticed.

Purr-puss seemed to be completely oblivious to our lurking as we bravely edged our way closer to see if we had come across something of benefit or something of harm. What we did not know was that Purr-puss knew we were there and thought we were just playing. She was not part of our dream day so she had recollection. To her we were her playful companions trying to surprise her. What great fun this will be to spring on them when they get closer; she was thinking.

There were four of us on that mission; Scout, Bill, Babbler and I. It is hard to remember, we did not know each other's name. We came to this conclusion of who was there when we shared our recapitulation of the events.

When Purr-puss sprang up we all went into flight mode, running in all directions. Scout, Bill and I found each other when the alleged danger had past but apparently Babbler ran all the way back to the tribe. He took back with him a new set of emotions that none of the others had experienced in this new life; excitement, fear, stress and doubt. True to his essence of babbling he squeaked and squeaked until Myra mouse was able to calm him down.

Scout, Bill and I Continued our unspoken mission as if nothing out of the ordinary had occurred. We forgot about Purr-puss's surprise attack as our stomachs reminded us of the task at hand. The successful discovery of food for the whole tribe brought back that carefree spirit that we all naturally had.

This experience brought about a shift in our group. Not everything was safe. Caution was heightened as if something could happen at any moment. The best way to put this in words (using hindsight) is "bravery was birthed". For the first time in these brief lives the factor of harm was lurking and had to be overcome. Forgetfulness and childlike happiness was the best tools for this as we found out.

Thinking back on this whole experience I feel that it was the lack of seeing our reflections that caused the tribal bonding that was so prevalent. We only saw each other so the realization of our own in-divide-u-all-ity did not come into our blank rational mind developing in that life.

As our brief life progressed and each of us used our natural essences to play and survive we had to change our developed routines with the change to our environment. Mary's ability to read minds and share her calm instincts was subtle but was the glue that pulled us all together at times. Myra's ability to heal by bringing calm through empathy helping healing also helped us in this lifetime. They hold stories within our story entry.

Starting over without existing concepts or influence from others who have conceptualized reality for us, caused old concepts to be re-examined and new concepts to be noticed. I see this clearly now that our memories have returned.

It took thousands of years to develop concepts. A his-story of man shows this. In this life as mice we lost all of the knowledge gathered from man's observations with limited perspectives. As the evolution of man progressed from hunters to gatherers or from gatherers to cultivators we kept our past instincts just adding to or building our paradigm. As we learned to communicate we gathered into families then communities creating structures for dwelling to help and protect one another. The verification process began early in development. In order for any idea to be implemented it has to be recognized, verified, agreed upon then acted upon. The ideas such as law, religions, governments, language and just about everything needed verification. Verification or validation of ideas developed into cultures. Mutually beneficial ideas caught on easily; like the idea of farming, while other ideas needed other methods of persuasion to achieve the validation or consent to become part of our existence.

It truly amazes me just how much we have defined into believable existence that has no true substance, with only beliefs holding them together. Even in this progressed society where the illusions of money, debt, governments and segregating belief systems are old dogmas we still box in our reality. This magical day with the mice has opened up a billion new possibilities to the realization of existence or source self-recognition.

Belief is one of the most powerful forces in our shared experience. The ones that are shaping belief systems know this. Your verification or validation or consent or ap-prove-al is like a gift of energy or exchange of energy.

Creating beliefs is like creating gods without realizing that you are the god creating a god, in a way; it takes your belief to make that god valid. Limiting beliefs brings illusions of substance and boundaries on possibilities. Although shared beliefs hold greater power or influence in our shared environment. We are the genie in the bottle.

Each one of us shared a recapitulation of our day/lifetime as mice with accounts that inspired this journal entry. Scout announced the intent of what they shared was to bring us all closer to "is" or "just being". He told us that it was important to them to not forget the minds that they had before Brandon had shared concepts and communications with them. The uncluttered mind is closer to source and they wanted to share this with us.

We thought we knew this but the true experience brings with it a state of being that we can return to at any time, to receive added perspectives in our observations.

One other reminder we all experienced as we discussed our lifetime was the development of our emotions. We had no names for what we were experiencing within therefore we had no de-script-ions for us to follow. A de-script-ion is a script given to us for us to act out. Without the de-script- ion of fear as an example; each of us had a separate reaction to the stimulus causing the body to re-act. Babbler ran around with the fear always with him after his experience with Purr-puss even if he did not know it was fear he was holding on to. Even with his feelings he was writing his own script. In this case it was a feeling associated with an event although he was unable to get others to act out his script-ion of what we de-scribe as fear. Scout, Bill and I each had the same encounter with Purr-puss as Babbler although we followed our own script. It was up to us how we scripted our journey without a script being written for us.

If we need guidance there are many scripts to learn from but we have to choose what script was act out when we re-act to anything. If you are acting on your own script then you do not need a teleprompter from someone like Babbler who may be holding on to his reaction to one event. You may want his story but not the script he has chosen to follow. You do not need a teleprompter following someone else's script.

Our descriptions of our emotions are limiting what we feel and how we react. Without the scripts to follow many paths are open. There are billions of ways to de-scribe the emotion love but it is unique each time with each act. E-motion is your action from stimuli.

This is just the surface of what we forgot that day/lifetime and it is hard to scribe the experience in limiting word descriptions. We shared a lot of memories of the forgetfulness.

Someone that de-scribes a remedy or claims to be an author-ity is looking to take you power away from you by writing your story or maybe they are just offering choices. It is up to us how our energy is used and what we spend it on.

I de-scribed this day as magical but a couple other "mag" words that fit as well. It was magnificent and it was magnifying. I am sure this experience will draw us back.

We ended this day after our long discussions looking forward to what the next day of our dream vacation held for us. Now we dream our dream sleep that prepares us for the coming experiences. We probable do not need sleep but that is how we de-scribed ourselves when we created this dream scape vacation reality resort. Is this cosmic fun; or what?

ALBERT'S JOURNAL OF THE UNIVERSE

7TH ENTRY

A DYNAMIC SHIFT

September 2nd-2045
Continued

In all of our experience with the Gateway, the world tour and this amazing dream vacation we were unknowingly preparing ourselves for what this day's gift would present. We have lived out lifetimes in the blink of an eye, we have traveled the micro universe as well as the macro, we have visited beings from our middle Earth and in far reaches of many galaxies, we have transformed into photons of light, we have explored our essences in many ways and there is no limit to what we can imagine. Yet somehow we were not prepared for this day as well as we could have, had we known it was coming.

The dream day started out with a surprise visit from the child I am presence that we met in Lemuria along with our old friend Zeb. They brought with them a marble small enough to hold in their hands.

Zeb de-scribed to us what this was; "what I hold here is a world seed. It is missing the ingredients to plant it in the garden universe where it can grow and flourish. This seed of life can grow roots strong enough to support the most bountiful fruits this garden universe has ever tasted. Although it will not look like what your con-cept of a tree looks like, it is similar to what you call Mother Earth or Gaia. All of the elements of this seed are there for you to nurture your intent as you will make up the final nutrient necessary for the celestial planting. A place in the galaxy has already been chosen."

The child I am presence continued; "just as I offered the life force of my 'I am presence' into the gateway we are asking that you do the same to fertilize this beneficial seed. You experienced a lifetime with the loss of all concepts teaching you what you need for this cosmic mission. Each of you will choose a single concept to bring to the free will beings that will inhabit this pearl in the heavens. You will not be able to manifest form to communicate your chosen concept although you will find that all the elements are at your disposal."

For many of us the choice was clear. Brandon chose the concept of language, Penny chose the concept of sound or music, Myra chose health or healing, Charles chose molecular awareness, Seth chose duality for some reason, Mary chose the concept of emotions, Bill chose the concept of unlimited perspectives, Scout chose the concept of societies (without the concept or knowledge of governments), Jasmine chose curiosity and I chose the concepts of time/space. Each concept has multiple sub concepts and we had no idea how our hints would be interpreted by a free will sentient (se-tenant)* being.

We could only respond to those asking questions and our responses had to be communicated through the natural elements of the world. We would be in the air, water, ground, fire, ether, plants and everything that made up this world seed. This meant that we would also be within each of these beings also and they just had to come to an awareness of us as concepts for learning to take place.

Jasmine's concept of curiosity spread naturally in brightest of these beings, it seemed to be openly present in most of the life forms although within what they named themselves "hue-el" curiosity was influenced by Bill's concept of multiple perspectives.

Hundreds then thousands of their years past before they slowly started to communicate. First through emotions and empathy and then by spoken language as they assigned sounds to have meanings, gave names to everything they encountered. They created scripts that could be passed from one generation to the next. Most everything was scribed by symbols or drawings at first then as language progressed the symbols were put together to represent sounds that held meaning that would place a script into the minds of those that learned language.

We observed as new interpretations of these concepts took on different paths of discovery and development. These beings were making it all up as they went along then seeking validation followed by replication to spread the script they were creating. Only a small minority looked into the heavens, tracked the cycles or became aware of the concept of time/space but most of the other concepts would eventually lead to this concept quarry.

*(se-tenant)- consciousness that is USING a physical vessel to live a lifetime experience. Hee-hee!

The hue-el beings traded equally among each other the good and services needed to improve their daily existence. The concepts of honor and trust were instilled in the script that they were creating although the duality of fraud and deceit showed great promise to a group of self-centered hue-els. This small group would prove to cause havoc on the development of the hue-el race.

One thing that stood out to us as concepts/ observers was that when beings get stuck or fixated on one concept it would cause a stall in the development or evolve-lu-tion* of that species. It is like putting a puzzle together ignoring all the pieces except the ones you are focused on. That puzzle will never be completed.

Many of the stuck in-divid-u-als* were masterful script writers that gathered multitudes of validators, re-confirming their incomplete concept conclusions. The validators found it easier to follow the scripts of others by calling them authorities or learned scholars. The validators only did what they were told and gave up the capacity to create concepts on their own. They only looked outward for their answers when more answers are within. Social classes were formed and those that did not conform to the scripts being written were harvested. Those that conformed to the script and acted out their role in the script benefited so there was no apparent reason to act out of character. They could not imagine the realm of possibilities that resided outside the limits of the script writers. They could not see the script for what it is (a small piece of the big puzzle).

The hue-el society became largely validators as concept creators dwindled in numbers to a point that they got ridiculed or shunned if con-form-ity to the written script was ignored. As a result to the complacency of the validators, society was developed with a limited perspective that only held benefit for the few script writers that slowly gained control of all the aspects that would allow for the whole of the race to prosper.

**in-divide-u-als- beings that seek validation of their own reality by coercing others with scripts of con-fusion meant to play to inner sanity of beings.

The script writers came up with the con-cept*** of ownership as they made claims on everything including ideas. This was rather comical to us because we were nothing on this world except ideas and they were making claims on us attempting to enslave or corner the market on something that is abundantly available to all. The validators were so entrenched in the script that they could not comprehend the folly of the ridicules claims.

Somehow this world was taking the same path as our home world Earth took in development and we felt that our roles in this world seed as ideas/concepts was failing, baring an unhealthy fruit in the universal matrix. What could we do to turn a world of validators back to their natural state of concept creators capable of writing their own scripts?

Generation after generation were programmed to the limited script as the script took on or absorbed the existing concepts of this now; self-imposed prison of limited possibilities. Validators became enforcers of the script agreeing with everything they were told. The only way to escape the involuntary imprisonment of ideas was to separate yourself from the closed minded society that was taking over the world paradigm. Then you could write your own script, then seek validation on your own or you could just write your own script as you went along integrating and respecting the scripts of others. This would often prove to be a path that if not recognized, would lead to hardships from the script con-form-ist. If you saw beyond the normal de- script-ion you took the chance of being de-cleared in-sane which was actually be enlightenment beyond the script. It was more important to be out-sane than in-sane. The script writers, programmers and enforcers could not allow inner sanity so insane became a bad thing to avoid. They just associated the word with harmful actions to program the desired result that fit the script.

What concept is missing? What questions are not being asked? The Hue-el's have to ask the right questions for the answers to come. We have no direct influence on this world seed. Even though we are limited to the concepts we choose for this playful mission we were part of the elements that hold all the answers.

***con-cept- the prefix Con in this definition is the higher dimensions of the heart/mind. This is where we make everything up. Create illusions that become real. Con-sciousness, con-cept, con-fusion, con-fiscation, con-stitution, Con- sent, con-fidence and other words with the prefix CON all refer to the heart/mind and in ways creation. Just as f.e.a.r. is just false evidence appearing real; our minds create. Therefore "con-cept" is a thought created by the heart/mind.

In the small village of Kraven in the valley of Plenty was a small child with the curiosity needed to start asking the questions that even took us as a surprise. He was named Zepeda at con-cept-ion as the Hue-el created a name for the possible child before the act of inner-action took place. This was written into their script at the beginning of the ages on this world.

Zepeda had a thirst for information that was not hampered by the limitations of the script writers. He learned the script and how the script came about. He followed the script writers back through his generations, looking back to the earliest scripts known. He looked at all the actors in the script doing their role without the hint of other possibilities. Zepeda became a script scholar that seemed to validate all that was written, taught, followed, performed or acted on. He also searched for old scripts that were destroyed by the script designers.

Zepeda was also quick to notice how the script was written to favor the script designers and held little advantage for the average validator. With all the determination and wit he could muster he set out to change the so called master script that should act-u-al-ly be written by all. The master script being pushed on society held only the perspective of the script designers.

Because the now scribed laws were being enforced by the validators it was not easy to step out of the script being claimed. Validators became subjects, servants and unknowing slaves to the script designers through sleight of hand and illusion. With honor and trust so deeply ingrained in the master script it was hard for most validators to realize that fraud and deceit could thrive in the master script.

One day after extensive travel and learning Zepeda returned to his village of con-cept-ion. He felt that a return to where his quest began would help with his questions. He saw that he began as a con-cept formed by his mother and father. Looking back he recalled how he developed, changed, was influenced by his surroundings and what he was taught. He also recalled his un-quenching thirst for data in this new realm of existence when he woke up as a baby. He noticed that the village had its own unique script although it was quickly assimilating to the master script. Because the location of the village was isolated, the programming of the master script was not as prevalent.

Our team of dream/concepts/ideas/elementals concentrated out essences in this village for Zepeda to tap into. We could only hope that he would ask the right questions.

Zepeda visited all of his favorite places from his childhood. While he was hiking in the mountains not far from the village of Kraven; Zepeda took off his footwear to walk along the banks of a stream leading into Lake Kraven that the village was founded near. After a deep contemplative hike he sat on a rock with his feet in the water. He looked up into the heavens reminiscing his whole existence, placing all he had learned into a nutshell he noticed that he had just begun learning. His thoughts were not mind chatter; what he was experiencing was more like a flash recapitulation.

This would be our best chance to relay all of the concepts that we had to share. We could not enter Zepeda as photons or sparks of inspiration like we have done on previous journeys. He was in touch with source and we were just a neural pathway traveling with the elements. This was his intent alone that would allow our sharing. His questions came 'one right after another'. With our limited assistance his answers came just as quickly. To ask, then answer all of his questions would take volumes so it is best to just get to the main question Zepeda ended with; what is my role, creating positive progressive change with my fellow Hue-els. There are many answers to this question and the answers lye in everyone. The answer that sparked Zepeda into act-ion was his passion for learning.

Then the un-expected happened, Zepeda spoke; "spirits of the elements I feel your presence. Show yourselves! Share your knowing! I am just a humble learner asking for friendship."

How could he know of us? This did not matter as all it took was his asking to allow us to share with him. One by one we made our presence known with Mary and I first appearing as photons of light that glistened off the water. Brandon, Charles, Penny, Bill, Myra, Seth, Scout, Jasmine, and the rest of the mice with us all came into form that Zepeda could relate to. His open heart allowed us to appear in the forms we associated ourselves with even though we looked nothing like Zepeda, except we were crystal base in our molecular makeup.

We communicated for several of his day cycles becoming great friends. We shared our experiences on our home planet Earth. Zepeda came with us into our 5th dimensional dream scape as we shared more of the wonder that the universe has. He marveled with us as we shared the planting of his world seed with him. He could see the potential for the bountiful blossoms that his world could offer. He felt the loving intent placed in the seed world as it was planted then nurtured.

Scout showed Zepeda that even his most fantastic dream of what could be was not only possible but with the dreams of others it could outreach all possible expectations. Accepting is better than expecting, there is more to learn with act-ceptance. Detached acceptance is even better, that way you do not have to validate or seek validation. Action towards others is taken only if harm is being generated, action is needed to stop the ill-ness that the harm causes.

Zepeda soon realized that source is everywhere and everything, experiencing itself from every perspective imaginable. How wonderful!! No script writer can trick, claim, force or coerce their limited perspective on anyone or anything, not without your consent or validation.

When the time came for Zepeda to part with us he had full comprehension that we are travelers just like him and not deities or prophets. The universe was now his playground. It took the source within him to ask the right questions so now his questions are more abundant than ever.

Zepeda spent the rest of his lifetime showing others how to look deeper for answers. He did not go out to seek validation for the answers that he channeled through his being; instead he just encouraged other to look at everything from as many perspectives realizing that we can never see all perspectives. He shared his learning but not as a script writer, he was more of a script integrator. He realized that inspiring was more beneficial than to realize the script but not turn it into a dogma that was deemed un-questionable.

Our task as concepts was complete now that the spark that Zepeda started spread. We observed as the seed world blossomed in the galaxy garden it was planted in giving out vibrational healing.

Zeb came back at the conclusion of our dream day/journey to share a further surprise with us; "not long ago Albert and I met for his first time in the city of Lemuria". "When we planted the world seed it was not planted in your linear time-stream". "It was millions of years before your Earth even existed". "This was my first meeting with Albert and you cosmic explorers." "In many ways we have gone full circle as you helped me at the beginning of my adventures I help you with your adventures." "Zepeda was one of my early manifestations in the universal hologram."

The hologram of agreed reality is as malleable as we can imagine. We can shape it however we like. We agree or validate reality into existence. What do we do with this knowledge/concept? Hummmm! I say that we should be mindful of natural law even as we learn to push the limits of natural law; our com-pre- hen-tion of natural laws may change but it still governs the universe

...tim; plummer...

This concludes journal entry for another day on our dream vacation that was created with shared experiences of our whole family of mice and man. Wow! And Hummmm! What lies ahead as our dream vacation is coming to a close? What fun!

ALBERT'S JOURNAL OF THE UNIVERSE

8TH ENTRY

ART AS A MEDIUM FOR REALITY

September 2nd-2045
Continued

This dreamscape that we vacation in is a product of our imagination along with memories from countless lifetimes. Each one of us played a part in the creation of this 5th dimensional reality. What a group tapestry of love and cooperation. The knowledge that our reality can be changed even re-created is clear to us all.

Like canvas with layers of paint; each layer is an improvement, until we get the desired look we are con-tent with or meets the satisfaction of our mind's eye (subject to more change). This dreamscape is an expression of our essences; therefore it is a work of art that we would like to share with those that may find enjoyment from  our perspectives. Recording all of our experiences in this journal is not de-scribing the wonder that makes up our malleable environment.

...tim; plummer...

The new dream day on our dream vacation was one of relaxation and appreciation. The whole group came together; all of us opened up our senses, taking in what our surroundings had to offer. This is our agreed upon reality with our individual perspective and essences. On our seventh day we rested.

As always I will fall short con-veying into words what cannot be fully con- veyed. The magic, the vibrations, the textures, the sights, the splendor, the detail, the natural flow of our colliding minds and what each of us experienced as individuals would take volumes of pages. So it is with wide/broad strokes on this recorder that I make journal entries.

In all of the ways that "art" has manifested it is clearly the second step we take on the bridge to reality. The first step is image-ination; the image or images, vibrations or sounds, thoughts or feelings: perceived by our con-sci-ous-ness. This is where magic (mage- ic) starts. Through "art" we create a path of sharing/legacy that leaves imprints on reality, with a life of its own. Whether the transformation from image-i-nation to con-vey-ance is through painting, music, literature, doodling or whatever, it now becomes something that others can pick up on easily if they choose.

The next step on the bridge to reality is acceptance, validation, consent, sharing or approval. This is where integrations/compromises take place as you believe you need support for the next step. It is as if you need validation that the ground or some other means of support is there if you stumble. Many be-lie-ve that to take this step in blind faith is foolhardy, others say it is divine wisdom. This is where your will power comes into play. Here is what designs the test-a-ment or product/consequence of your will power.

The third step is where your imagination is defined, described, placed into shared concepts, named, planned, molded, analyzed, acted upon or discarded. This step is where "art" is important as your image will start to take on a malleable form of its own. You may have to take this step on your own.

Albert's Journal of the Universe

Here in our shared dreamscape full of images taking form from vibrations that we all con-trib-ut-ed to; we all just wanted to appreciate each other's essences and this turned out to be an adventure on its own. For us to share this dream reality we need to con-struct an image that can be seen by more than just our team/family. That is the purpose of this journal, it is a rough draft that will preserve the imagination or images that we wish to share. By using the limited mage-ic of words to create an (i-mage) and casting a spell on each word by spelling it in a way that creates an image we can do magic with our i-mage-in-na-tion.

Bill's essence of observation went into playground mode as his child within came out to play. His child was always prominent although his playfulness is usually more subtle. Like a babe in wonderland his eyes met with every detail. His buoyant behavior caught on as he shared all of his re-discoveries as if he was experiencing it all for the first time.

Lights and shadows blended perfectly creating colors transformations from the micro to the macro. Vibrational energy emanated from everything as if our universe was singing and each object was responding in kind. The wind flowed through us whispering wisdom that could only be felt if you were open to it. We just experienced being conscious forces within nature so it seems only natural to start listening and feeling the elements as new gifts was presented to us.

All that it took was a glance of re-cog-ni-tion for anything to manifest. The flora and fauna was beautiful everywhere although when we gave our attention towards detail of a flower or insect new alarmingly clear perspectives came into view. Even the tiniest thing cast a shadow, re-turned our energy by re-sponding to our energy even if it was our shadow over powering the shadow they cast. The distribution of light gave life in magical ways.

We observed with appreciation, gratefulness, awe, wonder, love, acceptance and being. After all we were observing our souls/spirits manifesting into combined reality.

Something felt intriguing when we approached an energy vortex coming from a large cavern surrounded by a large layered granite shelf. At this point we all transformed into our photon beings to follow the vortex to its source. This vortex had both sides of a parallel line swirling down to its center. On one side of the line we were naturally drawn to there was the polar opposite of what was on the other side of the line. It all was returning to it source as one. Each loop in the vortex took us through a series of visions but also a wave of conflicting emotions. Each loop had its own vibrational tones. We gravitated towards the positive side of the polarities although we were close to center so we could observe the opposite polarity.

The outer loops of the vortex were spun tight with a long rotation taking what felt like lifetimes to circumnavigate. As we made our way closer to source the band widths of the vortex got further apart as the polarities mixed together still keeping a center line. We traveled along with the flow the vortex was taking us. It was like taking a tube ride down a slow moving steam with wonder on both side of the stream. On one side was wonder "wow" and the other side was wonder "why".

The tension between the polarities on the outer loops was also much more intense. The vibrations were scurrile, jeering, tightly strung and pitched at a high frequency. As the band widths widened the sounds became pleasant, more distinguishable. We have traveled many paths back to source although this one is approached with fresh intent as we just enjoy the ride along with what it has to offer.

We observed the progression of creation from a single cell to complex beings structured out of the elements in their environment. What we saw was limited to what we have fashioned from our combined knowledge. We again realized that we were stuck with the tools we had to work with even in this advanced dream world of endless possibilities. Maybe we will touch new memories that will enhance our tool box of data that we draw from.

Alternate time lines are just a fraction away as we make our journey. Straying from one polarity to another causes new timeline perspectives that affect your view of the stream. We stayed close to center most of the way although each of us witnessed events as they happen from the proximity of where they were in the polarity stream. For those of us that got within the opposite polarity the same event would have varying reaction that would slightly alter the flow of the stream from one pole to the other or more entrenched in the polarity they were in.

Linear progression showed us the extremes of our decisions and how those choices placed us in the multi-dimensional time stream of endless possibilities. The development of art along with the influence that artist have on any society became apparent as images of everything from cave painting and primitive drumming to master pieces of sound and sight. Art work appeared as species evolved as creators using material from surroundings. Most art appeared in nature from ants building an ant hills, to bees building bee hives, birds building nest, beavers building dams and even more sophisticated structures or portrayals of images from those that often copied from nature. Observers of natural design replicated images and usually failed at attempts of creating outside natural cosmic laws. Guidelines and borders were drawn by some that limited new art to judgment without the recognition of the divine source of the artist. If something did not fit the current mold of acceptance it was discarded as inferior. Renascence would take place as art became welcome in the heart centers of any beings.

Symbols took on meanings as interrupters gave fixed meanings to shapes. Many alphabets were formed where symbols represented sounds or vibrations, this would help form reality. Each culture had its own set of symbols that could form recognizable sound to convey messages or communicate. Shared validation would improve on the development of what we call language. This is an example of how art is transformed into a reality.

One thing we also noticed was that the transformation from imagination to some kind of shared reality fell short in the translation. In this journal alone are many examples of this. Even the most masterful word magicians or musicians lose bits and pieces in the transformation. This is mainly due to interpretation or perspective of the observer (who may be part of this sharing of images) as well as limited tools within the toolbox. How do you cage imagination?

Creations are formed in the macro world of imagination then brought into the micro reality, transported through art. It is said that the great wonders of man were formed in the heavens then built on Earth. The methods of building many of the ancient wonders of man are being realized in our dream reality vacation.

When we reached the source of our shared dreamscape vortex we already knew we were on our journey away from source taking with us the nutrients needed to make the journey through source essence once again, continually completing and beginning journey after journey. Source is within everything so it is everything from "I am" to the great "I am". We are the vortex, points within the vortex, and the source of the vortex along with both polarities of the vortex. We travel a path of unlimited [re]-cog-ni-tion.

We found ourselves back at our shared dream resort as if we had never left. We talked about the day's adventure as if it was life time's ago. Talking is just the word that I use although to properly translate how communication actually took place would be shared knowing or bouncing neutrons, shared energy, con-versing or telepathy. Spoken words are no longer necessary within our team; it is only necessary to convey our images out as art to be interrupted.

Each of us is holding on to our desired/divine essences as we transform continually in this shared chronicle. Layers of hidden talent within us are being un-veiled. The children are displaying abilities that are marvels of playfulness. Each of the team is bringing imagination to reality with tools of art that seemed impossible not long ago. Penny's sound creations manifest at a whim. Charles molecular abilities have just begun to glean the possibilities. Brandon has formed a bond with nature that only free communication can tap. Mary keeps the lines between us open as she shares her natural essence. Myra's healing energy is present on a cosmic scale. Bill was observing probabilities, possibilities or perspectives through the eyes of creation. His guidelines were limitless.

Our mice friends/family continues to surprise everyone with their grasp on reality in the world we are creating. Scout asked us some funny questions; "who came up with the con-cept of duality?" "If we are creating from past experience then duality is something that was made up, and then entrenched that image in our mind's data bank. How do we see beyond what we think we know?" "Are we watching re-runs of our group reality?" "What would happen if we void the con-cept of duality from existence?" "Would we view a completely different set of events or maybe just interpret the events we see without that perspective??"

All that I could say at first was; "wow"! "We will all have to look into the answers to those questions." "Our experience living as mice without pre-con- cieved con-cepts allowed us to see the wisdom in your thoughts." "Our e- motions affected our re-action with the instinct to not bring harm we were guided by new natural rules, governed by our connection to prime creator."

Bill chimed in singing; "now it is just something that I used to think I knew." He continued by saying; "duality is part of natural law with the concept/perspective viewed then defined by man." We cannot change natural law so when we observe natural law we can only seek knowledge" "As our abilities develop we could remove our scripts about duality but duality will still exist." "Geometric shapes exist within all matter that has natural law guiding them, without duality creation does not take place so we cannot take it out of the equation."

"The polarization of duality is where truth is;" Albert adds as the main point. "That went missing for a while in our society." "The frequency of truth being reached creates harmonics that shape matter." "By increasing our frequency are we able to transform reality even on a physical level." "Truth is described as a straight line in the center of a wave/curved line, it is both lines."

"This vertex that we experienced earlier showed us that the further we were from the centerline of truth the more chaotic was our experience"; Mary noted. "Myra rode the center line of truth the whole journey through the vortex." "The center is the truest path on the ride."

"By riding the center line of the vortex I was able to observe both polarities with a pleasantly comforting ease"; Myra started sharing. "This center line is where healing takes place so I was naturally drawn to it." "Charles must have had the most fun because he navigated the polarities like a skier behind a wake." "He also increased his frequency of crossing the wake as we went along."

With new ponderings ahead we simulated another day's closing with a well resting sleep. This was one of our favorite dogmas so we hold on to it. What is a dream vacation without plenty of rest?

Dreaming within a dream, within a dream! Is our physical reality a dream also? We can touch, see, hear, taste and smell because we wear a body that is capable of these functions. We have use of the body/vehicle to experience a shared reality with others. Trust with prime creator is needed; we are all extensions of prime creation.

ALBERT'S JOURNAL OF THE UNIVERSE

9TH ENTRY

FIRST CONTACT

September 2nd-2045
Continued

Our eyes opened as we heard a chanting of sounds, we symbolize with letters. Aaaaaaaa! Uuuuuuuu! Mmmmmm! We heard the word (om) that we attach to this sound while we listened to the vibration of each letter. We could see in an instant reality as we had created it come onto perspective. It was like turning on a computer and the data that pops up is what we programmed to pop up. The screen/background on our dream reality took familiar form. We felt the wind blowing across our skin as if it brought a message from another reality.

All the dream vacationers met in the dream-scape resort courtyard having been awakened with the same vibrational sounds. Everyone's e-motions were strong as we re-acted to the stimuli that we shared as we woke. Purr-puss and our mice family were already in the courtyard looking upward at lights that danced about with grace and purpose. They formed geometric shapes that flickered from one conceived symbol to another in the flash of an eyelid. Is there a message in this display that was coria graphed for our witness? Is this the answer to our questions about pre-conceived reality, shaping our surroundings?

Yet this was a typical first contact scenario that is part of our ingrained data banks within our minds. Small variations occurred with each of us individually although we all felt within our heart centers that we were being provided a gift of new awareness. This was our shared dream-scape reality but now we had more vis-it-or-s. These visitors showed themselves to us from within our dream universe. Their visit was short as we watched the visitors dis-appear as quickly as they moved around.

At first it was a validation re-action from our encounter. Did you see what I saw? Nothing should surprise this group with all that we have shared/witnessed together but we all agreed that it was totally un-ex-pect-ed.

The first thing we did was form every shape we could remember with molecular art (as we term it); which is just giving form to thought. Charles was a big con-trib-ut-er to this playful puzzle our visitors left us with. His ability to pull molecules from the ether is his favorite playtime. Penny recreated the sounds that we all heard with amazing accuracy. With her ability each sound took on a shape that Charles would give sustenance to the form/shape that was created. Brandon was the language expert in our group so he was instrumental with this puzzle gift.

Bill's ability of observation from multiple perspectives brought out many agreed validations on this witnessed event. Bill noticed that within each light was a form/shape that was hard to see unless you switch perspectives. These shapes are like the forms that we hold on to when we transform to photons in our journeys. In the center of our photon beings is our pre-con-ceiv-ed version of our vessel as if we are still the driver of this photon/energy vehicle.

We have never had communication problems with any beings we had come across in all of our journeys. This message was from outside our known existence so nothing made sense to us, as we relished the challenge, like playful children with new toys.

Myra giggled like a small child that has just learned the most amazing secret; she could not share yet with the rest of us. Myra always gleaned universal levities and giggled, so we did not think anything was new. To write this journal in linear progression; Myra's secret revelation will have to wait.

Using our abilities we re-created the event in every detail within our memory/data banks, then our image-i-nation played it over as many times as we liked at any speed we wanted.

Purr-puss along with Scout and tribe had the earliest memories of the shared/validated/witnessed event. Scout showed us his first contact by arranging our replicas as he witnessed coming out of a rift in our dream sky. Scout's theorized; "they did not leave through a rift so that means that they are still here in our dream reality". "Is it possible that they could return from where they came and never leave at the same time?" "The proof of that is the mark/print/message that is left for us to intrepid."

We are all aware of the endless possibilities for universes to exist just outside what we consider reality; we were vacationing in one of those time/space reality/creations so this was not hard to grasp. This visitation was somehow out of our realm of possible scenarios even with its similarities.

It took effort to scribe this event into something we could comprehend as familiar. One detail that we re-created was our e-motions/re-actions to the event as it happened. This defined the intentions of the visitors as we all agreed that we felt loving vibrations.

While Bill, Brandon and I worked with the playback of the light display to bring comprehension/meaning to the message the rest of our group took pleasure in the hunt for our new visitors. Seth and Scout took the lead as the best trackers in the group. They split up in teams with Myra, Shawna and Penny exploring with Seth. Mary, Charles, Scout and his tribe followed Scouts tracking. Seth tracked with the heightened outer senses using the eyes of the eagles and the ears of wolfs. Scout used his inner knowingness/instinct that comes from his heart center. Mary helped with cautioned logic while Myra followed a vibrational field that she was able to experience in her ability to heal.

It did not take long for us to pick up on a trail that would lead to our visitors. Mary took notice of a slight shift within the dreamscape reality we have been vacationing in that was not familiar. Myra commented that; "it feels like we are right where they are yet we still have to travel to meet them". "How can they be right here and somewhere else at the same time, unless they are dreaming also?"

Bill was the first to notice that the shapes of the lights formed ancient shapes and symbols found, then recorded on Earth. Brandon was able to read a message that said; "we are back, making it a time to remember". "Join us in this celebration".

We quickly joined the group of searchers with this new puzzle piece. What was to be revealed next was a surprise to us all as the dreamscape began to completely transform into a familiar yet forgotten scape of unimaginable beauty. We were now the visitors as our guest welcomed us with open arms reaching for long lost kin. The mice tribe climbed all over our guest stopping only to make embraces of affection.

Our new/old friends could see our bewilderment even as we felt familiar, our recall was not yet clear. They looked almost like mankind although physical shape was a subject of interpretation we could see genial connections to many species from our past memories. They also had old spirits in young children vessels that played with our children, it was magical watching this re-union.

As one of our guest who we remember as Lazarus whispered to me as we embraced; "how many times has this scene played out my dear friend?"

Without thinking my natural response was to reply; "too many too count." This was the truth that we were realizing as we flowed with the new tide. The memories returned to us all quickly although the scripting/writing of our multi layered time loops may take some effort.

We should start with Lazarus along the soul group we were again a part of. They were all familiars to us. Lazarus twin flame was Presence, they conceived four child vessels for kin that wanted the gift of a fresh start after a lesson was finally learned. The children were known as Essence (whose empathy nurtured inner guidance), Harmony (whose vibration could alter reality), Connell (whose natural being is helping the universal mind/consciousness) and Logan (who brings the spirit of free will as the master of natural law). They played with our children who all wanted a mantle for their names so Charles became (the substance of molecule formation or the formulator), Penny wanted to be known as (the image maker) and Brandon went with (the translator) as he was not really into the whole "mantle" thing.

Scout just stuck with his mantle "Scout" because that says it all. Among the mice tribe only Belcher wanted to be known as Belcher (the indigestion).

This part of the journal is playful fun as it is great seeing role essences played out in this dream universe. The play ended as we were invited into a structure of grand imagery for nourishment. The structure blended in with the dreamscape like camouflage. Lazarus opened a pathway saying; "welcome to our shared dreamscape". "The best way to show this home is by telling you that you will see what you wish to see". "There are energy vortexes everywhere so make yourselves at home".

As we entered Charles would say; "look at that, and that, and that". He still shared his new discoveries with us all. He treated everything as a new discovery. We looked at what he pointed out then validated it into existence. He would come up with a name for what he saw and we would agree most of the time as we laughed concepts into being. Charles favorite starter phrase is; "wouldn't it be fun if ..." The ... could be anything that would take us anywhere. "We could call it a contributor, or a converser, maybe we can name it an object materializer". Charles know that the name game was just for grins and giggles, so he took pleasure in the levity of names. He still had the jester side of his energy. He was a million year old in a five year old body, it was great.

I get carried away from the journal when I write about my soul family group. Getting back to linear progression of events or a blow by blow version of the flow of time. Our immediate surroundings were full of life, we were at mission starting point on a grand experiment with mind boggling variables, yet we all felt a tremendous feeling of accomplishment being there.

In order to tell this it may be important to say where and when we had traveled to so we could meet our visitors that took us in as guest. We were back on Earth over a million years in what we construe as time. The Earth was a jewel in the universe much like the world seed we nurtured while on this vacation. There was a bee hive of activity as most were excited because the observation satellite was soon to be moved into orbit around the planet. The new satellite would be called the Moon and it would record the development of the great experiment. What we thought of as meteor craters are in reality blast ports that helped position the moon into orbit around the Earth. They also served as observation ports for the study of living life, this was just beginning for many within the known universe. One of the many cosmic schools was soon to open.

This planet had the largest variety of biological life within the Milky Way galaxy so it drew the interest of many being with scientific inquisitive essences. The Earth had only a slight tilt on its axis, so the polar icecap were smaller. One could hardly notice the changes in seasons. Most of the planet was still a water world that allowed life to flourish in unimaginable variety as well as size and numbers. Only the continent of Pangaea rose above the waters. This was a large island land mass that sprouted evolution, producing beings of all shapes adapting to the environment.

We had visited Pangaea before in the city of Lemuria witnessing Lemuria rise into the heavens to become the Comet Nibaru. Almost the center of Pangaea was the garden of Eden where new beginnings were emerging that leads to the time loop we are on. Information on Pangaea was almost  instantaneous as many of the advancing beings taped into the conscious neural pathways of Gaia herself. Information is passed through the elements for all that carry receivers within.

At this point in Earth's story we were the visitors observing the indigenous inhabitants on the planet. One species captured our curiosity as observers, they lived in a frequency much different from ours so they interact with the physical world in ways that we are not familiar with, worthy of study. They possess a connection with source creation that holds many possibilities, ones that we wished to comprehend at a greater level.

They were curious about us also passing stories from one generation to the next through cave drawings.

Each area of Pangaea was influenced by many throughout  the galaxy. Even with the excitement of the moon placement into orbit there was an underlying tension among the aliens for domination of the planet. Not all of the alien races were on Earth with good intentions. The reptilians were using the indigenous people of Pangaea as slaves to mine gold and other minerals. They also performed genetic experiments that altered the DNA of the people stunting their growth and blocking their path towards source creator. This intervention was considered a violation/intrusion/rape by many of us others there to study or observe. This DNA altering made the inhabitants better slaves because it retarded the inner guidance connection with source, so they became disconnected with Gaea neural system. It was like numbing the body to operate so the mind does not receive the message of the pain being inflicted.

Now many of the species that they had altered were off the natural cosmic grid (so to speak) making them unable to communicate. The center for DNA altering was a development called Babylon. Once the manipulation/retardation was complete the specimens' would be divided into groups of colors or characteristics then sent to learn in schools that taught spoken words of different variations. Competitions were set up and encouraged that further separated the connections these people had with each other. Babylon was an expanding indoctrination facility producing a slave mentality that this world would have to fend off and this would take a millennium of cycles to do so.

Those that excelled in the indoctrination phase were elevated to positions of what is dubbed "authorities" then placed as teachers, rulers, guards, statesman or anything else that claimed power over others. Psychopathic behavior was rewarded with additional knowledge which helped maintain the slave population that was quickly emerging on Pangaea. True learning was hindered at every turn.

As a way to counteract what the Reptilians were doing, many other schools of higher knowledge were set up around Pangaea. Atlantis along with Lemuria have the best results helping the plagued victims

Albert's Journal of the Universe

of the Reptilian manipulation return to a point where inner guidance could begin its journey back to source creation once again.

Gaea herself was not pleased with the manipulation that was causing harm to her offspring. Atlantis was developing in harmony with Gaea although there are fractions of the population in Atlantis that had intent of war/destruction in mind. Technologies have reached a point that they could cause harm to not only Gaea but the fabric of the physical realm. This beautiful jewel called Gaea/Earth was being muddied with the prints of beings from all around creation. We could see that even with our non-interference mindset that our influence held the potential for bringing harm.

The path was clear for us as a soul group. The memories of the contracts we eagerly agreed to in order to help stop the harmful intervention taking place on Gaea. Was our life mission/contract fulfilled? Are we graduating from one school of learning to move on to an even higher school? We are seeing the macro universes plan come to fruit; it was indeed time to celebrate.

Every one of us has lived thousands of lifetimes over a million years with all of those memories returning to us as if they just occurred. Now we are back at the beginning, this is where our contract ends. One thing was clear was how our soul family always found each other in each lifetime. We had even been bitter enemies in some lifetimes. Somehow we made it back where a new beginning is clearly in our path.

Lazarus reminded us that we have been a part of a large mind/computer simulation that has played out millions of ways. These simulations are meant to come up with the best way to help stop the interventions taking place on Pangaea. They are designed to uncover veils of illusion offering greater clarity. Each simulation was just as real as the next as they all played out at the same time.

Lazarus spoke to the natural world net: "Now we welcome old friends back to what some call 'Prime Reality' which is part of the

Omni-verse". "We celebrate the soul group that has completed life missions that brings them back here with us."

Mary spoke for us all when she replied; "we thought 'Prime Reality' was back at home where we have a pool, where the children go to school and we play at our work." "Seriously; we are just on a shared dream vacation so we are making this all up." "It is great fun and all, although a quick dunk in the pool right now could be just what the doctor ordered."

Looking at the natural neural pathways on Gaea light up with laughter, was a sight to behold. Zeb showed up with Iam just as the celebration started. Even the elements joined the singing, offering vibrations that would be mimicked by birds from then on.

Mary pulled me to the side whispering; "Albert, this is fun but what I said is how I know we all feel". "My knowingness is validating all we are experiencing, as it happens with discernment". "Remembering that it is all a simulation that we made it all up, is still hard to grip."

She then smiled as she wisped me across our imaginary dance floor.

We spent the rest of our dream vacation in Pangaea with soul mates form every known corner of existence. We witnessed/validated many adventures with our remembered family. There is much to share in this journal. As you may have noticed when reading this journal, there are billions of stories within each story.

With the knowledge that we are just a part in a simulation it is now clear that we can choose to play a different role to complete the simulation contract/guidelines. There is so much to learn. How wonderful is that?

ALBERT'S JOURNAL OF THE UNIVERSE

10ᵀᴴ ENTRY

MISSION REPORT

September 2nd-2045
Continued

The celebration of our successful return to 'Prime Reality' lasted into the wee hours (if there is such a time). Recounting these events in linear progression is the best way to bring comprehension into view. Our team of vacationers kept to our learned schedule of rest; we were reliving a forgotten era in Earths story so time was moving at a pace we easily adjusted to. In fact the days and nights were almost always twelve hours with only a slight variation. The planet still had its equinoxes twice a year with only difference of one half hour on the cycle. Everything now is in remarkable balance.

This was before the building of pyramids. The remaining structures from this point in the time stream are not recognized as building in our normal perception. Many architectural designs were made to help correct the consequences of what we are reliving/remembering.

Lazarus shared with us a kind of mental debriefing helping us better comprehend what was happening; "we are reviewing what has already occurred, with a fresh perspective". "Thank you for playing this out with us from your added viewpoint". "Many are remembering, much like you with your soul group although few have stretched the boundaries of creator's self- realization awareness as your team of imagineers". "As you see we are quickly approaching the point on this path where Earth begins many dramatic changes". "You may recall that many things were taking place at the same time while the Moon is being placed into Orbit around Gaea/Earth with everyone's excitement and anticipation"?

"It will take thousands of years for these changes to happen and at this point nothing can be altered." "Just enjoy the ride through time/space." "You may also recall how the excitement of having a permanent observation satellite turned to concern as it altered the tides and orbit of Mother Gaea". "This would help lead to the separation or breaking apart of Pangaea." "Changes also happened over thousands of years that led many surface dwellers into Middle Earth where almost all species that have ever developed here on Gaea have weathered the storms of life".

"Perhaps the most damaging thing to happen in this period is the introduction, encouraged development of psychopathic behavior into the indigenous inhabitants". "With a developing mindset going on in Atlantis along with the attempts at DNA enslavement research being implemented, this period is making some important realization on cause/effect".

"Many of the visitors from all reaches that came to Gaea found the indigenous inhabitants attractive, then found ways to interact with them producing new ingredients into the DNA mixing bowl" "We discovered we could enter their life forms as it just began life to live among them". "The price was forgetfulness of who we are". "This reality held many advantages we cherished so we made the journey often into vessels where we learned their ways". "You are here after thousands of lifetime while you are still living a life on Gaea in what you feel is your 'Prime Reality' so this is nothing new".

"It is because you are both here and also in vessels riding on Gaea at the same time that makes this so wonderful". "You are a part of an on-going simulation". "Only Myra has visited us before, she brought your group along this time". "The only place to make change is where your vessels are in time/space". "When you return you will take with you all that you remember".

We all heard Myra admit that she knew who the visitors were when they arrived although she had no idea we would be witness to all of this again.

Lazarus continued with the mind briefing; "These events as you may recall are what led you to sign the contracts where you all agreed to live out those thousands lifetimes". "Just observe what you remember with detachment, be thoughtful with caution by thinking only with your heart".

This is what we did as a soul group, we traveled down memory lane together recalling early life events from our unique perspectives. It was not just remembering it was reliving in an instant. We took it slow at first as we re- familiarized with our provided surroundings/pace of life. We were back on Gaea's neural net so that was a lot to take in. What helped us the most was our past journeys as elementals on worlds created in our dream scape!

Each flower had a story that we shared, each rock, each leaf on every tree, all the critters, the wind, the sky all had a shared story that we connected with at a level we had forgotten. I cannot tell you all the stories in this journal so listen to those stories when you get a chance. No technology can hook you up to Gaea's net so this was a remembered experience we enjoyed. The net was a buzz on Pangaea as each story blossomed with new opportunity, hope with action towards life that was granted by source creator. Wealth was not even a concept yet because there is plenty.

Not all was well on Gaea's net as some have justified a self-proclaimed need to control, this brought an un-easiness/illness into the net. They lose connection to the net with this (ego) infliction, although the virus is still spreading, energy is high. Talk in Lemuria of plans to take the city off planet to tour the heavens is busheling on the net, as soon as the Moon is fully operational. This journey for Lemuria would not occur for another thousand years. We kept our knowledge of what we knew to allow events to flow naturally.

The whole team got refreshed from taking a few moments to reconnect with Gaea. We all got together for a group story time. Each one of us has experienced these events from a unique perspective sacred to our bond with each other.

Our mouse friend Babbler was bursting with questions; "call me dense if you like but I am having a hard time keeping up with what is happening". "Where are we"? "Maybe I don't have the memories this far back"? "I remember my life as a mouse in the tribe of Scout, I remember the fantastic journeys that we have been on along with what we have learned but now I am lost". "Why, what, who, when and how"? "I do remember agreeing to live my life as a mouse in the tribe of Scout, before that all that I recall is a burst of light from what we have learned is the central sun". "I remember billions of us lining up to go to this special place to live out life in a time of promise". "I did not know what a mouse was so I thought I was getting a deal". "No regrets, mind you, we have been on quite a ride".

"Slow down Babbler". Scout was the one that always helped Babbler when he began his ramblings. "I picked you for my team in that pre-life reality". "You stood out among those billion of new photons ready for a promised journey to Gaea's re-birth". "What you see is the story of Gaea as we have experienced our lives here". "You are a new spirit from Source Creator so this is all new to you". "It is your gift to look at this with fresh insight". "Relax, go with the flow, your insight is in your questions". "Be happy you are a mouse, I have lived as a hue- man and it is not so wonderful".

"We have all had different pre-life experiences that bring us to where we are". Myra shared her past experiences with Lazarus; "this is all about healing". "Everything we are witnessing is for us to better comprehend the source of an illness that has festered for a million years". "In our lives back in Utopia 2035 we have conquered aging along with all the illnesses known to us on Gaea". "Here we are grasping at what immortality really means". "Even Babbler who is 'a new spirit' has no true beginning or end". "Our real journey will begin with the sharing of gained wisdom from these sojourns". "For some reason the answer to all that plagues the cosmos is within our grasp making it a playful task to uncover". "Even the collective universe seeks nourishment".

"Our 'Prime Reality' in 2035 is changing each minute as more have reached their inner potential". "There are parallels in both time lines". "Gaea's natural neural net is actually active at a level we are not even aware of'". "Let's take the rest of our dream vacation learning our role in this cosmic healing".

This was something we all agreed to, after all it is us as "all" that we want to heal. What a wonderful intent. Back on Pangaea what we may consider magic was just tapping into natural energy that is all around. Massive dinosaurs' roamed freely as the order of life was presenting creatures that ravaged on other life for survival. Not known to the dinosaurs was an extinction plan that would wipe them out entirely. This was planned and orchestrated by a group from some other galaxy that did not like the danger that these creatures caused so as judge and jury they sentenced the extinction of the dinosaurs through bombardment.

Memories of these diabolical plans remind us we only had a limited time to save as many species as possible by moving them into middle Earth or Gaea's womb as many call it. Millions of beings lost their lives for the convenience of a few. As above, so below as those that survived on the surface mimicked this psychotic response from being above them by seizing the spoils, exploiting the weak. It took the combined efforts of Atlantis along with Lemuria to bring growth back. This was our first cosmic disaster where we began questioning the intents of our fellow visitors to Gaea. At this point we still did not know of the effects our Moon observation satellite was having on Gaea.

Gaea was scorched by the deliberate meteor bombardment with a slight wobble on her axis. Her skies were filled with dust and poison. Only the constant currant from Gaea's central atmosphere would clear up that mess. Still it took thousands of years to heal. With the renewal of life came many changes. Life was adapting to the new environment after the bombardment, the weather changed as winter made its way into being in places that used to be tropical. The wobble was creating a new challenge for life that it eagerly adapted to.

Everything was smaller, even man was tiny in comparison to earlier man. He stood more erect to make up for the loss in stature. This was a new breed of man, more intelligence towards programming making a bountiful slave population. Also with the potential for reaching boundaries way beyond those that plot to enslave. This new man was also attended schools of higher learning in Atlantis and Lemuria achieving insights that even stunned their teachers.

War was brewing among the star visitors with Gaea destined to become a battle ground, the indigenous will surely mimic the concept of war. Small quarrels that may have appeared to be major battles occurred, until peace was finally agreed on. These small battles appeared in the skies as un-imaginable magic of the gods.

The indigenous inhabitants were slowly being released from the master/slave relationship as a new golden age arrived on Gaea. Samaria, Atlantis, Lemuria and Eden were all major space/dimensional ports bringing cultures with higher learning to share with each other. Many in the remote area of Pangaea had little to no learning that shared a worship of the star cities.

The Anunnaki held themselves out as saviors, promising to bring order to Pangaea with their benevolent leadership. As observers we knew that many of the problems in Pangaea were the result of Anunnaki manipulation. We stopped their advance towards control at this point in time.

Ancient Mayans were the record keepers for the star gods along with many in portions of Pangaea that stewarded what would later be called Africa. Man was in a tribal stage of evolution as they found safety in numbers. Most tribal groups had a chief of sorts although the Shamans were relied on the most. We would usually communicate with the Shamans when we visited the indigenous beings.

Tens of thousands of years have passed since our arrival in Pangaea. We would soon be witnessing the next extermination event on Gaea/Earth. With the shift in Gaea poles along with a period of little solar activity Gaea was moving into an ice age. Glaciers pushed their way across the land shifting the shape, redistributing boulders the size of mountains. The added weight of the ice caused stress on Gaea's tectonic plates. The ice was holding the land together so when this great ice age ended, many shifts took place with the continents beginning to split apart making many inland cities (such as Atlantis) sea ports.

The bombardment of meteors, the orbit of the Moon observation satellite, the great ice age and the melting of the ice all contributed to the recipe for the biblical flood that wiped out most life yet again on Gaea. For those that we could not save by moving them into Middle Earth/Gaea's womb, we helped store the DNA of most species in Arks that were built by many indigenous being on Gaea. Lemuria made its journey into the heavens before most of this happened, with Atlantis eventually sinking into the ocean.

Atlantis was protected from the giant ice glaciers but could not do anything when they began to sink. It happened very quickly with only a small handful preparing for the event.

This brought us to the beginning of our mission contracts which is ten thousand years ago. First we mapped out a healing grid in Gaea where energy vortexes were centered. This was like acupuncture points on the body. We then began helping with the construction of pyramids that would draw energy form the cosmos to help with the healing process of Gaea.

Our efforts to help break the cycle of civilizations rise and fall is joined by many in the cosmos. The Orion's had a plan that would transform the cycle if man reached a level of awareness that would allow mankind back in the playing field of prime creator source.

With all that Gaea has been through there were only four races of mankind left on the planet. A tribal meeting with these races took place with the wisest in each group representing their clans. It was decided that each group would represent each of the four main elements. The groups would study their respected elements until they became masters, then the tribes would meet back together to share all they had learned with each other. The red man choose the earth, the yellow man chose air, and the dark man chose water with the light colored man choosing fire. They split up to different areas of Gaea to begin their study. More of this story is told later in this journal where you can see the answers that this effort provided.

The Anunnaki's influence grew as they claimed the mantle of gods. Solomon from the Anunnaki lived among the indigenous for thousands of years teaching way of manipulation that would become unquestionably dogma for most. The Anunnaki and the Reptilians jockeyed for power and control of the slave race called man. Things were no longer out in the open so they rarely revealed their true origins.

The history/her-story of Gaea was written all over with records from the past nine hundred thousand years removed from teachings. It was taught that this was the beginning of times for man on this planet. Only the wisdom keepers knew the real story and they were stifled, eliminated, persecuted or just ridiculed for speaking the truth.

For the most part Gaea was finally being left alone as many of the star races returned home. Only a small group remained behind. Our soul group was mainly from Pleiades with our family/familiars' choosing to stay and help Gaea on her healing path.

On all of Gaea's wisdom she agreed to allow the Moon orbit her celestial body, even with the added turmoil that it caused in her waterways. In many ways it helped with the development of life so it would be allowed to remain. It also helped stabilize Gaea's wobble as she orbited around Sol.

The earlier Pyramids in Egypt marked the center of the Earth. This is where the geometric ley lines would stem out from. They were built to receive or send energy back and forth to the Orion belt where much needed help was offered in the path to recovery. The Orion Nebula is said to be the origin of life in our galaxy. Nebulas are where suns and planets come into being/born so naturally this must be our creator. Who created the Nebula? We all have our own theories to that!

The vast network of pyramids along with oblast serve as power sources, transporters as well as interstellar communication. This energy was given freely from Gaea intended to be available to all. This was one of the many reasons for the great history/her-story cover up. One of the planks/guidelines for control is to control the distribution of energy. This is only one of the planks as many have been developed, implemented and accepted even in our lifetime back in 2035.

We all remembered agreeing to begin our life journeys fresh with no recollection from this point on. There must be a way to return these beings to a path of healing. We could only learn this by trial and error so running the real life simulations with billions of variable could only be done using the universes heart mind creation simulator or some may call it the heart/mind of creation. We hooked into the matrix of life on Gaea. The Akashi network where all knowledge is available to us.

As time speeds forward our journey slows down a bit with our continued rebirth into forgetfulness; life time after life time, begins. The mission goal in our spirit contract is to find our (mankind) way back to source. We are no longer Pleiadians! Even with our return here where we found our roots, we hold on to the simulations that brought us to this simulation. Each lifetime was a lesson, some lessons took many lifetimes. The learning process is endless. This quest to heal our miracle existence is part of our essence.

Mary giggles like a small child as we relive our first lifetime after the contract was agreed to. She and I were born as twins to beings that did not know any language. We answered to the sounds that our parents made. Mary answered to Ha because they would look at her and say; "ha". I became known as Err. When I would wonder away they would always make the sound; "errr". If I did not answer it would

cause an angry dance that could be very frightening.

For the most part these primitive parents were wonderful providers/protectors. Brandon (our language expert) was our grunting father figure, he answered to sounds not words. We were never sure what to call our father. High pitched noises usually got his attention. Mother was Myra with her being called; "Ahh", in this lifetime.

Somehow we communicated as we learned what caused us harm and what brought pleasure or satisfaction. The habitat we shared was under a waterfall with a natural pool inside that received streams from above with smaller drain holes leading into the waterfall. This was a constant source of fresh water that we swam in regularly. We learned to stay away from the vortexes that were caused by the drain holes. We did not know what a vortex is, so we just made a gasping sound when referring to the swirling water. We held our throats to further convey the message we were communicating. In fact if you came from another village you may think that we just loved to dance and make jesters. We got good at messaging, even with strangers.

One day we got a visitor to our waterfall cave from a being that seemed to radiate with knowledge, even the spoken word. This ambassador from Samaria wore strange clothing, he rode on top of an animal, and he made lots of noises that only he seemed to comprehend. He made fire with rocks and sticks, he trimmed his hair and beard with a sharp tool, and he had a string tool that could propel a shaft and one that could make sounds. This wizard shared his learned magic for a stay in our habitat.

"Ha/Mary" was renamed Joy with my new name of Get (short for get back here). Our Wizards name was Mer. He called our father Sir and our mother became Grace. He told us he named our mother after the feeling he got after Sir was done with him when they first met.

Mer took a special interest in teaching us as children. After we began to comprehend Mer, he would tell us stories that brought back memories in our forgetful life. Mer would point up into the night sky saying; that is where we are from and someday we will return.

The greatest thing that Mer taught us was how to make observations/ to learn on our own with the information that is provided to you. "Everything is your teacher". He pointed out nature's routines, the bees making honey, the deer returning to the same watering spot, the birds building their nest and so on. Only through observation along with imagination can you learn on your own.

"The gift of speech has a price"; Mer would say. "This price is limitations". "Names along with spoken description bring limitation that only you can overcome". "When you comprehend this, your learning will truly begin".

Recapitulation of previous lives is much easier from an outside perspective. This particular life had great significance in our development. For now this entry of the journal is concluding. We have traveled through almost one million years in a day so it is time to rest. Actually in our prime time-stream in 2035 only a few minutes have passed, although we are still in need of rest.

ALBERT'S JOURNAL OF THE UNIVERSE

11TH ENTRY

DREAM A LITTLE DREAM OF ME

September 2nd-2045
Continued

In this journal we have experienced dreams within our dream-scape, this is the first time that we would share our dreams with our previous beings. Mer (our wizard friend) turned out to be Seth. While in our sleep we all met with our living beings from this ancient period. Memories of the impact this dream had was vivid, so this was not an intervention but a reoccurrence of the natural Bow of this time-stream.

We met our doppelgangers face to face to encourage them on the mission/contract they had just signed into. This meeting could only take place in an alpha dream reality, we hoped this meeting would not be forgotten when they woke up from their slumber. As it turned out Mer, Grace, Sir, Joy and I (Get) woke from this dream with feelings of determination although they did not fully comprehend the meaning of the dreams they shared. Mer chronicled the dream on an old hemp parchment that he carried with him in hope that it would be discovered by future generations, reminding them of the mission/contracts they had agreed to in their pre-life. Mer wrote in the ancient Samarian text that he was taught in this life.

Mer carried with him many parchments that he stored in our waterfall cave habitat. The parchments have a story as well although that story will have to be told another time.

After our dream sharing, Mer told us of a land where wild life was plentiful, where people traded their plenty with each other, offering a greater variety of goods. This land could be reached by following the mountains till you got to a valley between two peeks then following the river downstream in the direction that the sun travels. You cannot miss the structures that are there marking your destination. Four sided structures of equal surface that join at a peek. It is told that these structures would take you into the heavens, return you to where you came from.

Sir did not want to leave our waterfall habitat but Grace, Joy and I (Get) could still get his attention with pitched pleas. Mer agreed to steward the waterfall habitat while we journeyed to this paradise. This may have been the first real estate deal in history/her-story. Mer now had possession of the waterfall habitat with the agreement that when we return we would take back possession. Little did we know that we would not return for many, many years?

Our return would bring hardship, bickering, quarrels, violation/violence and even death. While we journeyed, Mer fixed the waterfall habitat to his comfort, he met a beautiful spouse who bared him three children. His spouse was called Glory, they named the children Opus, Beth and Atlas. The wonderful waterfall habitat was now called Mer-land.

Our parents Sir and Grace were old now, tired from our disappointing journey. We had found the city paradise that Mer told of in his story although the way into the heavens was blocked by perpetrated ignorance, false misleading stories and guarded by brutes with pointed shafts. The alleged path to the heavens had been hijacked by a band of control hungry psychopaths with the intention of claiming this gift as theirs alone.

Mer was away when we returned. He had left on a mission to procure granite rock that would be used for building additional space just outside the waterfall on the  shores of the river leading away from the falls. His new familiars were aware of the agreement Mer had made with Sir, although they did not agree. Opus, Beth and Atlas had all been birthed under the waterfall and have lived here their whole lives.

Glory (Mer's elfish wife) has made claim to all the land visible from the vantage point that the waterfall cave provided. This alleged claim stretched miles down the river with the forest on both sides. She justified her pitiful compromise by "allowing" us to camp in what she considered her forest. Grace was very influential with the growing populace within her claim, as they had made this bold claim many years previous, making deals with travelers that would be void if they knew the truth. Glory used her elfish magic to keep tabs on us from inside our waterfall habitat.

This truth could not be known so a campaign of support was started. Promises of land gifting were made (as if Glory actually owned the land) to persuade others to follow her word over truth.

Glory came to us with a proposal; she would allow us to stay in her forest by her waterfall habitat if we agreed to accept her as land owner making homage payments to her alone and her siblings.

How could Mer be attracted to this manipulating con-artist? We did not have the words to describe the injustice we felt. Even the word that we found were claimed as knowledge given to us with a price. We did not know that Mer was adding a price to the agreement we had that allowed him to stay with us. The words he taught were claimed so you could not use them against the gift giver/teacher/author. What is happening to this world? If we went back to our old ways of communication using grunts, jesters, and movements/dance we would be ridiculed as primitive animals.

Mer would not allow for all of this twisted logic if he were here. Grace, Sir, Joy and I anticipated his return, where all would be made right.

When Mer returned, he visited us bringing with him a group of twenty men, adding to his newly acquired illusionary status as monarch within Mer-land. His new deal was not any better than the deal Grace was proposing. It was actually worse because he wanted a pledge of worship for bringing what he called civil-iz-a-tion.

Sir went berserk, reverting back to his primal learnings, lunging at Mer with clenched fist. He made noises that we only heard when we had done something wrong, only now he was out of control. He could not speak like the rest of us but he still knew right. Witnessing wrong against his familiars was too much for his already heightened sense of protection, coupled with frustration.

Mer's guard dogs quickly stopped Sirs justified attack with the pointed ends of their staffs. Mer has taken our waterfall habitat and now our father (Sir). Joy, Grace and I made Mer a counter offer; tell the people the truth, quit making these ridicules claims of ownership, help us work to create something that we all can make use of together. Use your learned skills to contribute not control.

This counter offer was out of the question as we were grabbed/kidnapped then held as prisoners. Before Sir was dragged out; Mer took his dead hand, dipped it in the blood then placed a print on one of his parchment scrolls. Sir had finally (in death with sleight of hand) agreed to give everything to Mer. This man we thought was a friend was now an enemy, he was like that vortex in our waterfall pool that we learned would cause death. The word enemy was new to us although we were quickly grasping its meaning.

We were lowered into a pit that had been hollowed out. There was only one opening allowing light in. The opening of the pit was too high to reach. The floor was wet and muddy with rounded walls impossible to climb. We survived on bugs, small critters and little fresh water. We had to apologize to Scout and his tribe for eating their ancestors.

The youngest of Glory and Mer's children called Atlas did not feel comfortable with how we were being treated. He had visions of a rule of laws he would create that would guide disputes to equitable ends. He was guided by inner wisdom; his family considered him misguided. He stuck to his passion by writing down what he felt the maxim of law should be. These laws would guide all other laws.

With all his good intentions he failed to realize that natural law is not written but it overrides anything written by man. Mer's parchment collection was now becoming a library. Glory would twist many of Atlas's inner revelations to fit an agenda more conducive to claim makers.

Meanwhile Grace, Joy and I withered away into shells of our former selves. We could see the stars through the opening in the pit as we looked up at them wondering when we could return and get out of this backwards prison we agreed to come to. One night while looking at the stars a basket was lowered into our pit, we were encouraged to climb into the basket. The basket was lifted up then it became our boat as we were sent on our way down the river to lands unknown to us.

It was just Joy and I now as our mother Grace did not survive the voyage in the river. When we finally came to rest on the shores of a lake with no end we climbed out to be greeted by clubs and spears. We were now prisoners of a new clan of man. They were new to us anyway. The remains of our mother were taken also, she was placed on a alter, then burned.

This clan (our captures) were not as advanced as we had become. Our arrival was magical to them. We Boated on the water, our skin was pale with our hair a different color, we spoke in different sounds, had knowledge of fire along with experience with nature. Joy and I were now the teachers that this clan held in reverence. This was much better than being prisoners in a pit full of despair.

Many came from all around this area to hear our teaching. We told stories of our waterfall habitat that was now denied to us. We planted seeds of retribution where we would one day recapture our waterfall land. In many ways we built the society that we wanted Mer to build with us, one that had no status claims or misguided manipulations. For those that listened we encouraged them to follow the inner guidance from our center. The only real worthwhile lesson that Mer had taught us.

Each clansman/woman had a natural essence that we helped them discover. This essence always brought value to the clan. The clan gave freely of their essences knowing that it would make them all better off. No one was held as being better or worse as we all have value.

Joy met a clansman that was quick to learn, she took special interest in him, calling him Adept. They soon joined as family after their attraction to each other grew into a frenzy of shared e-motions, bringing new life to the clan. I found a mate that had a link with nature that marveled my instincts. We called her Empathy. This was a good time for us as soon more were added to our growing clan. Joy had two more children (a girl then a boy) after her the joining ceremony with Adept and the birth of their first girl. Empathy gave us four boys that grew so quickly into men. All of our children heard our story of the waterfall habitat with the cunning Mer.

Our first journey as Err/Get and Ha/Joy ended peacefully. Many of our fellow clansman are in this soul group. We always found each other from one lifetime to the next. Memories of Err and Ha have been long forgotten, if not for this dream recapitulation they may have never held any significance.

This story of the Clans-men and Mer-land continues without our spirit participation. The Clans-men eventually invaded Mer-land in a mis-guided attempt to right a previous wrong. Natural law is obvious; two wrongs do not equal a right. Mer-land was better off with the Clans-men so the universe was made better in a small area and a brief moment after the redemption-invasion. The corrupt ideas in Mer-land twisted good intentions into tools of manipulation, so who won?

The life of Err and Ha made it into the Akashi records like all other stories that were going on. This story repeated over and over with only slight variations of names, times, place and circumstance. It all starts with someone making claims that in natural law are comical at best. We do have a natural realm that we have barrowed for a lifetime (our bodies) that should never be trespassed without our full knowledge and consent, this is true with everything. We should not trespass on others. You cannot return to the heavens with items you acquire here on Gaea. You can image them into being, once in the heavens, if you still feel a need.

Claiming ownership of time/space/land/air/water/fire/speech/ideas is the mentality of bully/cowards. Soon we would enter the age of trust as many bought new meaning to the word "breach".

Sir had a TRUST agreement with Mer. Sir was unknowingly the GRANTOR of the TRUST as Mer became the TRUSTEE with Sir and our family as the BENIFICIARIES of the TRUST. Once Sir became a BENIFICIARY he was no longer the GRANTOR.

Mer was clearly in breach of TRUST, the claims of ownership of the lands, waters along with all that he could watch over was another breach of man-kinds TRUST as stewards of Gaea.

We watched in amazement as even the concept of TRUST that has the root "TRU" in it could be manipulated into a tool of control,

105

by some. This became a new catch as the position of TRUSTEE was GRANTED by a higher GOD/AUTHORITY with their Bock of followers as alleged BENIFICIARIES, which have no "say so" in the TRUST agreement. The GRANTOR is no longer available but here is the document that proves it, on this magical paper. It says so in the literature we give you to read. TRUST us! We are divine, blessed with divine knowledge passed on through our heritage.

Give us your belief so we can capture your spirit. We can use your spirit as collateral when dealing with other psychopaths. Governments and religions used TRUST agreements to gain control of the people without closure or consent.

Gaea's people were spread out around the world. The red tribes were split by the continents splitting. Man would not meet up with many of their red brother and sisters until the rediscovery of what would be re-named the Americas.

Most all alien intervention is done behind the scene with many veils of illusion to get through to them. Masters appeared in different areas in many timelines as man progressed once again remembering their star heritage.

The attention seeking, psychopath prospered in this bizarre world as profit was slowly becoming the active deity that most people worship. Lifetime after lifetime went by, way too many stories to tell in this journal. Methods of extorting energy from others was turned into an almost deniable fine-tuned instrument.

For the most part everyone went around unaware of any manipulations, while perpetrating the manipulations along. The rise and fall of regions around the world were just part of the grand experiment. Currency became the rulers as alleged Kings, Queens. Monarchs, Dictators, Emperors, Religions, and Corporations, States or governments of any kind all sought its inBuence. The controllers of currency controlled the world. These controllers created TRUST agreements to use as collateral. The alleged plantation landlords

(Kings, Queens, ect.) all knew this as they struggled to increase their Bock, therefore raising their imaginary status.

One only has to look at mans' history/her-story to see the conBicts this causes.

Government census is just an inventory of stock for trading purposes, masked as a way to see what the people need the most.

Everything was working like a fine crafted watch until the birth of mass communication that took place in the lives we are living now in 2035 using the Gregorian time clock.

This recapitulation dream that we are experiencing is taking us through to the roots of what causes failures to great empires, Joy and Get started with ideas that developed amongst the red man before the return of the eastern inBuence. Our family of star-beings met up in another story of great relevance on this quest for healing of Gaea. This has become an all-out effort to break the cycles of decline, creating a lasting path toward growth and evolution. We have become "cosmic matrix script writers".

Many lifetimes went by before the next major learning experience in societies hope for thriving presented itself. The Hopi Indians held great inBuence in many alternative timelines. In our next experience the group of dream vacationers would not reveal themselves until the galactic intervention from the Hopi spirit Maasau. This life as a Hopi Indian would shed light on our now cosmic mission to bring about new cycles; as healthy, compassionate source creations with never before realized potential.

The first memory that I have in this lifetime as a Hopi Indian in the deserts of Arizona was crying for breath in a new surroundings. My birth took place on a center of power emanating from the great-spirit. My awareness was peeked, my senses were heightened, my parents were nurturing balls of energy with a physical form in the center that they could use to interact in the three dimensional realm we are gifted to be in.

...tim; plummer...

This story should be told as another journal entry. The visit of Maasau with the return of Maasau about to happen again in our 'prime reality'. Our family of souls all played a special role that will illuminate answers on this cosmic quest before our dream vacation ends.

ALBERT'S JOURNAL OF THE UNIVERSE

12TH ENTRY

LIFE IN AN ALTERNATE REALITY

September 2nd-2045
Continued

There are many alternate realities that exist at the same time. Billions of alternative simulations have been running simultaneously. What we consider "prime reality" is the one that we interact in, even if it is another parallel than the one you just left or the one we are living in now.

We would jump into one of these parallel timelines on occasion as we went from one life into another with minimal briefing between death and re-birth. This life as a Hopi Indian was not in our current timeline history/her-story. Some of what happens here has created changes to our "prime reality" as the Akashi records all timelines. Much of this story is also part of the Hopi legends, so some that read this will be familiar with the legends. This is told because it is a key to the answers we seek on our journey. Healing society and not repeating a destructive cycle.

This story is told from my perspective as is most of this journal. I was female in this life. Living life as a girl/woman/goddess has amazing lessons that are part of the path to source. They called me Moonbeam, my birthing location was gifted with a sliver of moon lights on that place of power.

My father was a great Hopi shaman called Souring Eagle. My mother was Patch-a Momma. They lived with the planet as well as on the planet. They even knew that we were traveling through the galaxy on a planet starship called Gaea/Earth. They knew all about Gaea neural network of communication along with our connections with other star beings, stars, galaxies and alternate realities.

Needless to say, this was a wonderful family to live a lifetime with. Even though I was feminine, the hunter/gatherer was my essence/play. Staying with the tribe elders getting water or making clothing were necessary lessons although the magic of the earth, air and heavens was my drawing passion. As a small child Souring Eagle would share his wisdom while I listened with impeccable recall. He repeated his stories a lot so that helps with the re-call.

The tribe had no concept of greed as each provided for both themselves and the tribe. The task was clear; to live in harmony with nature. This was the best example of how man could live natural law. The tribe functioned like a single living organism that provided healing on a planetary body. Many have said that it takes an entire tribe to raise a child and my father would say; "it takes an entire universe to raise Moonbeam". Note; My Hopi dialect is not that good so we will continue this journal complete with translations [as usual].

With Moonbeams connection to Gaea's net came floods of information. Only the guidance of our family helped get this overwhelming gift within a container that was flexible enough to grow as the matter with the container grew. My family gifted me with a pouch that should always remain empty of matter until you called upon what you needed, reached into the pouch and it would be there. I could even pull light out of the pouch to illuminate the darkest of nights.

"This gift is from the star beings", my mother told me. "Maasau has visited many times". She would point to the three stars of what is known as Orion's belt telling me; "that is where Maasau is from, he told us about you". "Somehow you are a player of importance in the cosmic plan". "You and your spirit group will unite here in this lifetime to meet Maasau". "He said; 'your dream path will be clear'".

I could feel my excitement all over as she told me of this 'spirit group'. Moonbeam's mind seemed to meet with mine as she replied; "they are already with me, I just haven't met them yet".

So far she was sure that Souring Eagle, Patch-a Momma and possible our best friend re-named Hummingbird, (as he always darted from one object to the next, he would hover then dart) was in the 'spirit group'. It was as if Hummingbird was absorbing information from everything, then moving on.

Moonbeam wondered who else may be a part of this 'spirit group'. White- cloud could be in the group also. She can imagine things into being using what nature/Gaea provides, she does not have a pouch like mine but she sees potential in everything to become something else. The clothing we wear are products of her natural alchemy. Maybe Red-feather, he tracks like a mountain lion with his senses on full alert. He has taught us to observe nature without judgment, everything has cycles, even the skies where our star brothers come from.

When Maasau first reveled here is when the stone tablets were created with the meeting of the four races that (with assigned tasks) dispersed in the four directions, this was ten thousand cycles ago. He has only visited in the most sacred dream ceremonies since then. Would his visit be in another dream vision or on a more physical plane that can be witnessed by many?

No time to ponder who may be part of this 'spirit group' as Moonbeam realized that they will all revel themselves in the event. There was much to learn in preparation.

The Hopi had a way of recognizing then dealing with psychotic behavior, that is an infliction in man that can be avoided with simple knowledge. If the infliction is allowed to fester it will upset the balance of the whole tribe. This mental imbalance occurs in man from time to time, so it has to be treated.

The behavior that this infliction brings, is easy to recognize. As soon as these behaviors show their ugly heads it causes a sharp wave in the energy patterns that surround us. This wave could pierce the fabric of reality if left unchecked. The dis-ease spreads quickly making the environment unstable. No one with this mental infliction is placed in a position of responsibility or allowed to force authority. That would only bring harm to the tribe.

Pity was the normal response to those inflicted with the harmful behavior of the self-proclaimed command of "lesser beings" or natures gifts. These delusional notions of self-centering ego are simple not accepted. They are ignored as if they do not exist (only in the mind of the inflicted). Any true leadership is earned through positive action.

For those with this illusion AL feeling of wanting control, it stemmed from a feeling of fear/chaos. Some of these behavior patterns can be almost unrecognizable except for the most trained shaman. Each of us are susceptible to this disorder and it is best to be able to see it within yourself then make the corrections within also. When it becomes visible to others is when things get challenging. That is just natural law so the disorder has its own cure if we let it and not nourish it.

One symptom of psychotic behavior is when someone takes what is provided freely (such as information from the Akashi or elements from nature) then uses these to barter. This also starts with a ridicules claim of ownership. This is "MY" idea, or "MY" land, or "MY" water.

Mine, mine, mine and if you give me yours I will give you a portion of mine. The Hopi would just laugh at these claims and that is why the white man (when he came to our location) had to resort to violence/violations.

Another natural law is; one solid object cannot occupy the same time/space as another. We just barrow the time/space as we move. Usury of time/space cannot be violated without natural consequences. Natural law has its own means of enforcement. Trespassing on another time/space has consequences.

The Hopi children were encouraged to retain that connection with creator that is natural. Natural law was the biggest lessons to learn. The wisdom of natural law is common knowledge among the Hopi. This is more important than assimilation to Hopi ways, speech or social programming. If the spirit is in line with natural law then they are naturally beneficial to everything.

Observing Moonbeams life from both her perspective and mine is enlightening. The rest of our team already know who they are in this lifetime I am experiencing as Moonbeam. They have chosen not to reveal themselves to me at this point.

What happens in this life as Moonbeam is way before the arrival of the white man. In this time stream, many things happen that did not happen in the 'prime stream' we are part of back at the USE lab. The variations bring man to blossom with creation at a quicker pace.

Deceit/lying was also a symptom of imbalanced psychotic behavior. Once your truth was broken with the Hopi tribe, you had to go through a long period of reflection that left you on your own. To survive this period one had to return to their center then come back in truth where they must remain to be balanced.

There was no stealing going on here either. Not everyone had a nice worm bear skin coat or good moccasins for their feet but if the need arrived these things were shared equally. If you wanted a pair of moccasins for your feet you could learn how moccasins are made then make them for use or trade. Information was shared. Each child was taught the crafts that they needed.

Not all bear skins came from killing the bear; bears die naturally also and they gift man with the warmth of their skin way into the afterlife. The exchange of energy is recognized with gratefulness.

When a child reaches the cycle of adulthood they are given a journey to complete. You must return to the village with proof that you have completed this journey. Each task was different for each child passing into adulthood. For Moonbeam the task was to bring back a feather from an eagle, the skin from a bear, a flower from a hibiscus bush and a vine from the banyan.

This would take Moonbeam south to where these plants were abundant. Moonbeam took her pouch with her although it could not be used to manifest what she is tasked with.

The bear skin was Moonbeams first task as she may need the added protection of the bear to complete her journey. It is preferred not to kill a bear on these journeys. The dangers of intruding/trespassing on any bears are clear to all. It is best to gain then honor trust with the bears. This can only be accomplished through connection with Gaea or gifted from Gaea. Taking an unnecessary life is out of the question.

Moonbeam climbed up into mountains where bears are known to migrate. She watched from a distance at a family of bears fishing in a fast moving stream. The fish seemed to jump into their arms or mouth, they were so good at it. Moonbeam had nothing the bears might want or need, how can this be done with an equitable exchange? How can balance be maintained? These were the questions that plagued Moonbeam while observing the bears.

As Moonbeam pondered this, one of the smaller baby bears lost their footing on the slippery rocks and started uncontrollable down the river in Moonbeams direction. She acted quickly grabbing the limb of a tree while reaching for the baby cub. Her timing was impeccable as the cub flowed right into her open arm. Moonbeam could see the look in the family's eyes as the baby cub ran up to her parents. The mother bear looked Moonbeam straight in her eyes with a spark of appreciation.

The bear skin was Moonbeams task of the earth, the eagle feather was her task for the sky as she kept her eyes towards the horizon at all times so she could see both land and sky. The Eagle feather is a contract with nature also, it takes an honorable spirit to get one from an eagle. Many find their eagle feathers on their journey although it is important to Moonbeam that the feather be given freely from the eagle.

The hibiscus flower is a task of the fire as it owes its very existence to the sun as does everything else. The hibiscus however only thrive where the sun and water are plentiful (tropical climates). The vine of the banyan is the task of water as the vine brings water to the branches and leaves of the tree. All the tasks are dealing with the circle of life that is all one. Many interpret their tasks the way they want to. Moonbeam would have to travel in the four directions to complete the journey.

Meanwhile she had reached an unspoken relationship with the bears. Moonbeam stealth fully followed the family back to their cave. The night on the mountain were getting colder as winter would soon be here. It is much better if you are in the south when winter comes. Moonbeam camped close to the den of the bear family. They would start their hibernation soon where they slept all winter.

The bear family knew I (Moonbeam) was there and tolerated my presence, because I helped the cub they did not feel threatened. Moonbeam learned to fish from the bears although she had to modify the technique to fit her stature. Thanking each fish or berry she found recognizing the cycle of life.

Each night Moonbeam would build a fire then hold her personal ceremony with the intention of tuning into Gaea's net. She had no feelings of loneliness as she had contact with her guiding spirits that connect her to the universe. One connection she made was with the small critters in the area.

Moonbeam made friends with a couple Chipmunks that stayed in her area.

She called them Tip and Tap because one would tip things over and the other would tap on things with curiosity. After a bond was created, Tip and Tap would often snuggle with Moonbeam on cold nights. They learned quickly not to tip or tap the fire then learned to appreciate the warmth that the fire gave freely.

Before the hibernation of the bears began, Moonbeam saw a very old bear leave the den. This bear looked directly at Moonbeam inviting her to follow. This bear seemed to know what Moonbeam needed. The bear allowed Moonbeam to follow him into a large cave that appeared to be a graveyard for the bears. Bear skins were everywhere. This old bear has come for his last hibernation in the cave of bear spirits. All moonbeam had to do now was ask the bear spirits for the gift of warmth from what they left behind.

Each bear skin held bits of energy from the spirits that had lived their bear lives. Not just any skin would do. The energy must meld with Moonbeams then permission from the spirit or previous user must be granted. Only one bear spirit stood out among the selection. This was a gentle spirit of small stature for a bear but fierce as a force of nature. This spirit matched Moonbeams essence so with pure intent Moonbeam asked; "oh great bear spirit I ask if you will journey with me, in exchange I will bring back to life the vessel you wore in your time on Gaea. You can continue your life journey with me if you choose".

The bear spirits reply was; "you will have to clean me up to look presentable".

Moonbeam showed gratitude to the bear spirit along with the old bear that led her to this place of honor and power. She took her gift to the river where she cleaned it. Then she laid it out in the sun to dry. Moonbeam used a blade to cut the skin to fit her stature and cut access into strips that would be used to mend/sew the skin tighter to her frame. She made moccasins also to protect her feet. When she put her new coat on she could feel the merging of spirits with the bear. With this added power she would finish her journey.

Following the mountains Moonbeam headed south. Tip and Tap were now her traveling companions. They rode on Moonbeam most of the time, climbing around her like she was their own moving tree. With her eyes peeled on the horizon she panned the landscape as well as the sky. Moonbeam spotted many eagles although most were too far from her to make contact.

On top of a high ridge overlooking the forest that Moonbeam was traveling through, she spotted an eagle nest. The climb would take her way out of her way and be very treacherous. Tip and Tap would have to wait her return at the base of the ridge. She would ascend the ridge then make connection with the eagle.

The bear skin was too cumbersome to maneuver in so she left him with Tip and Tap. It took Moonbeam a complete light cycle to make the climb, she would have to spend the cold dark cycle without the comfort of her bear skin or a fire. When she made it to the nest the eagle was out hunting. There was five eggs in the nest that must have sensed her arrival as they  began to open. The mother eagle could not count so when she returned she had what she thought was six hatchlings. One of the hatchlings was strange compared to the others although a mother's love can overlook that.

With the chill of the evening the mother eagle took all of her hatchlings (including Moonbeam) under her wings for warmth. Moonbeam was surrounded by feathers and she only needed one. She would need the Mother eagles consent to take even one. This eagle was large even compared to Moonbeam who was much bigger than the other hatchlings.

She chanted all evening a song that soothed both the mother and the hatchlings. One of the hatchlings followed Moonbeam around the nest like she was her admired older sibling. They formed a bond that allowed moonbeam to see through his eyes. Moonbeam stayed with the eagle family until it was time to be taught to fly. The mother eagle pushed each hatchling out of the nest over the ridge where flight was the only salvation. When it was moonbeams turn to be pushed out of the nest she backed away from her mother eagle chanting Gaea's song of harmony. The mother eagle plucked two of her finest feathers then gave them to Moonbeam as she edged her out of the nest. Somehow moonbeam knew that the mother would not let any harm come to her.

With one feather in each hand she fell like a rock. The mother eagle caught Moonbeam before she hit the ground. Her siblings all landed around her offering support. The sibling she had melded with promised to stay with her until she could fly. He was growing strong quickly so he felt he could protect his grounded sister. Moonbeam called him Guardian.

Tip and Tap were in fear of Guardian when they first met. Guardian saw the attachment his sister eagle Moonbeam had with the chipmunks and respected the friendship.

Two of Moonbeams task were complete as the four of them headed south once again. Moonbeam could see all that Guardian saw, so finding paths through the mountains became much easier. Winter was here to run through its cycle making for cold nights.

One day as they traveled Guardian spotted a large animal that appeared to be injured. Moonbeam recognized the animal knowing it was a horse. She approached the horse with caution speaking in a soothing tone, holding out an apple she got from her pouch. As she got closer she could see that one of the horse's legs was swollen as if he had taken a bad spill. Moonbeam wrapped the sore leg in mud along with some healing plants she had learned about from Souring Eagle. They would stay with the horse while he mended.

After a few days cycles the horse pranced around without even a limp. That is what Moonbeam called him (Prance). Prance was almost fully recovered so he let Moonbeam, Tip and Tap ride on his back for spells as their journey continued. Prance eagerly joined the entourage on the quest.

With Guardian in the sky and Prance on the ground the traveling became much easier. They would make it to the land of the hibiscus and banyan by spring. The forest was slowly turning to jungle as plant as well as animal life was enriched by the sun and rain. Everything was in abundance, Flowers grew in fields like the sand in the desert, and millions of flowers covered the land in the open fields. Moonbeam observed how balance was maintained. The wind, insects, animals and birds all played a part in propagating the plant life as the plant life gave back as nutrition for the animals.

Our Spirit group of dream Vacationers watched in wonderment as Moonbeam worked with Gaea.

ALBERT'S JOURNAL OF THE UNIVERSE

13TH ENTRY

VISIONS OF ENLIGHTENED SOCIETY

September 2nd-2045
Continued

Along the path to wisdom we meet many other spirits that are learning also. These spirits take on many forms. Tip, Tap, Guardian and Prance chose to be with Moonbeam even without the knowledge of the whole scope of her role in this life.

There were many Banyan trees around her now although Moonbeam has not felt the invitation from any of the trees that would allow her to cut a vine from them. Hibiscus flowers are abundant also, not just any Hibiscus flower will suffice as she looked for a divine Hibiscus bush with sacred origins.

One day as moonbeam was traveling with her companions she heard a large roar coming from the sky. From out of the clouds a large flying metal bird with fire coming out of its underbelly headed towards them. Lights flickered all around the metal bird as it landed in a field near Moonbeam.

The bird opened up a giant mouth after landing. A beautiful woman came out of the mouth. She walked towards Moonbeam carrying a gift. Then she spoke to Moonbeam; "what I am going to give you is a prize that has a sharp edge. It can be used to carve out the most advanced society known, or it can cut the ties that bind men together laying waste to man". "How you use this gift is up to you". "I am called Ixchel of the essence LOVE". "Many have mistaken me for a goddess although I am just a star sister here to help man".

"Here is what you will call civilization". "The structures you see on this gift were created by man with the assistance of my star brothers". "They only represent the wonders of mans' achievement, the true gift is love that will bind the civilization together, without love, man will destroy themselves leaving the structures behind". "This gift of love is already within man, what I offer is what is needed to cultivate that love so man can use civilization as a benefit".

"You have been chosen to deliver this gift of love to the Mayan civilization that you soon encounter". "They teeter on the edge of returning to the stars or destroying themselves". "We wish for them to come back into the cosmic fold".

Moonbeam could feel the sincerity in Ixchel. Is this the destined meeting with the star being Maasau using another name?

"I am not Maasau", Ixchel answered Moonbeams thoughts. "Your destiny awaits as this is just a passing moment". "The gift of love is your natural essence, you need only remind the Mayans' of their true nature".

"Place this gift of civilization/ becoming civil in your heart center knowing that violations of natural law is de-civilization or uncivilized". "Anything that is not centered in the love vibration will only bring harm".

Ixchel returned to the metallic bird that took off with a roar of fire. It moved so quickly that it was gone in an instant.

Moonbeam put the physical representation of civilization that Ixchel gave her in her magical pouch. The matter vanished once inside the pouch. Guardian took flight to search for the structures shown by Ixchel. Moonbeam joined Guardian in his minds' eye seeing all that Guardian sees.

From the eagles' higher perspective the "civilization" was easy to spot. Guardian made one pass through the skies of this city of man. Moonbeam could not comprehend the amount of negative energy permeating the air. Energy was all chaotic. At one point stones were thrown at Guardian in an effort to bring us harm. These malicious motives/negative energies are contrary to "civilization".

The city was not far, Moonbeam, Prance, Tip and Tap would make there on land by darkness. Guardian found a roost where he could view how man behaved gathered in massive numbers.

They entered the Mayan city with ease, visitors are welcomed here as a guiding rule. Moonbeam quickly noticed that this was a mixing bowl of energy vortexes carrying power from all over, to mix in with the Mayans'.

Each man/woman had their own culture (with the defining syllable "cult") that they desperately held on to. Most inhabitants seemed to be stuck or stalled by all the con-flict-ing energy generated. Moonbeam's path was clear; she went in search of the city's Shamans. She would know them when she sees them.

Many Mayans turned to look at Moonbeam with her animal friends. Prance walked side by side with her. She did not need any types of restraints as Prance was with her of his own free will. Tip and Tap ran up and down Moonbeam as they walked along. What a sight for the children, they spotted her better than the adults.

The marketplace was crowded with people. Many shops had food from many places. One shop had beautiful birds all caged in decorative styles although you can make slavery look nice but it is still slavery. Buying or selling natures beings for personal gain made Moonbeam cringe. What kind of place is this?

As they neared the housing habitats a small dog was being thrown about by an irate man. He had no use for the small dog so he threw him out. He was too small to eat, so in a way that saved his life. He was lucky that Moonbeam saw the whole event. The small dog was injured from the abusive treatment he had just encountered, yet he perked up when he saw Moonbeam. Help had arrived, his instinct knew as he wagged his tail with excitement. Moonbeam placed the small injured animal in her warm bearskin after treating his injuries. His will to live was amazing as he mended, he would be called Willy Willpower. The Chipmunks cuddled with Willy as he rested. They shared their playful energy with him.

The now enlarged team of journeyers found a wise Shaman in a place for drink. He did not hold a position of importance with the people as Moonbeam expected. He was alone, alertly watchful of his environment. His attention was drawn to Moonbeam as if recognition had pleasantly alarmed him when he first spotted her.

Stories were shared even with the vast difference in their spoken languages. Communication was more of a projection of visions from one mind to another. This was like Moonbeams connection with Guardian.

Moonbeam visions showed her how this ancient city had come to be in the state/condition that it was in. Cultures were loved and welcomed with only one rule of law. That rule of law was high jacked by man as the disorder of contrary behavior infiltrated this fine city with those that could nod wisely while speaking stupidly. Many play at being a Shaman, so the high esteem of a shaman is held by impostures. Any true shaman would not dabble in manipulation for personal gain.

The remaining record keepers here all await the harvesting of this prison, as the reptilians feed on this negative energy. At the time of the harvest some of us will return to our star families.

The shaman spoke verbally; "This harvest is not necessary, with your arrival it can be altered, many more of us will return home in the heavens". "You have the gift from Ixchel to bring to the city". "The words that she shared can turn the tides, so we can all move on".

Moonbeam agreed to stay in the city for two cycles of the solstice or one year before returning to the Hopi. In this year many changes took place in the Mayan city. Moonbeams stories were shared by all with the ending catch phrase; "in order to be a Civilization we must first be civil".

Natural law was re-introduced as the only law. For those that suffered from illusions of power or control over others, they were finally becoming unacceptable. Most of them changed when reminded of who they are, and that the universe provide an abundance of energy. They did not have to take energy from our fellow beings in this shared existence. Communication improved among the many cultures. Common denominators created a new culture that allowed for individual culture to still be nurtured. Culture/dogma was no longer a 'cult' but a cherished uniqueness.

A new paradigm had taken root in this society, in just one year. Trust had to be earned, proven with thought then action. The natural TRUST agreement we have is with nature, should be honored as the PRIME TRUST. This TRUST was our contract we made when we agreed to take part in this life experience. Our second TRUST agreement was with our parents (who do not always live up to this TRUST). The next TRUST is with society although if society is already in breach of PRIME TRUST then freewill allows choice. Breach of TRUST is not worthy of support/energy. The most powerful TRUST we have is with ourselves; this is the one that determines if we will honor anything. This is also the TRUST that determines the perimeters of any TRUST.

The bully mentality quickly became impotent, slithering away into the dustbins. Energy given freely without force or coercion is sacred and the universe has an abundance to share.

The shaman Versatile became close to Moonbeam in this transition time. The city was healing quickly. Soon, Moonbeam would return in her final direction on her own transition journey. Before she left she was given a beautiful hibiscus flower preserved under a see through shell that is air tight. The flower would maintain its beauty and not wilt. She was also gifted with a braided rope, made from the strongest and biggest banyan tree in all the land. The gifts came from the people who heard Moonbeams story, also from the plants who produced the value. Moonbeam was grateful to all!

There was a great crowd there at Moonbeams time of departure, many witnessed her place her gifts in her magical pouch, then seem to disappear. These magical events that were so natural to Moonbeam became the start of legends. They left the Mayan people in awe and wonder.

Little Willy Willpower returned with Moonbeam, Prance, Guardian, Tip and Tap. Versatile would come to visit them with the Hopi Family.

Willy was the early warning sign of anything new. He would dance with Tip or Tap, barking and panting then place his tiny head on them hugging them for the playful banter.

His perky ears with sensitive nose had him in constant surveillance mode.

His ability or super power was spotting danger. If there is no danger, he would bark and show his bravery. Once he stepped on a leaf that stuck to his foot, he growled franticly at first, shaking his leg to get it off of him. When he finally got the leaf off his foot he ran around the leaf barking, he would lunge at the leaf then draw back giving bark commands. There wasn't a leaf in any forest that would mess with Willie after he was through. With real danger he would just growl in a whisper tone.

On the path back, Guardian warned Moonbeam of a mountain lion that was tracking them, anyone of the small critters would make a good appetizer for this animal. It is best to avoid confrontation with caution along with prepared awareness. Willy was on high alert as usual, in his mind he was the group protector although he played as if nothing could happen.

The travelers used shadows to mark the direction they would take. As always, Guardian would fly ahead to find the easiest passage wrought. The mountain lion used the shadows in a different way. He/she moved within the darkness of the shadows to stalk his/her dinner. The lion moved about the trees and forest stealth fully, quietly approaching the small group of travelers. His/her movements were hard to follow although Willy was always the first to notice the lions close proximity. A whispering growl followed by commanding barks alerted us as the lion made its move. Moonbeam stood firmly grounded as the mountain lion circled them. Tip and Tap hid themselves within the arms of the bear skin. They would jump out as feral chipmunks for surprise if needed.

Reaching into her pouch, Moonbeam spoke with comforting certainty; "you look hungry my feline friend". She pulled out a fresh fish from her magical pouch; "here, this fish is ready for you, this is the fishes' higher purpose, it needs to move on". "Our time is not upon us yet, only you can determine if it is your time to move on". Moonbeam gently tossed the fish to the Mountain lion who only took a moment to devour it. Her piercing eyes never left Moonbeam. Willy was in whisper growl mode.

Pulling another larger fish out of her pouch, Moonbeam continued her TRUST agreement with the mountain lion. This agreement would need both parties to act as GRANTORS. The mountain lion would grant safe passage then he must become the TRUSTEE of the TRUST to insure that the TRUST be carried out. The BENEFICIARIES are Moonbeam and her companions. Moonbeam was GRANTING the same safe passage for the mountain lion with Moonbeam becoming the TRUTEE.

The TRUST contract was settled with the acceptance of the second fish acting as SETTLOR. Tip. Tap, Prance, Guardian and Will were all witnesses. They were all cautious with the mountain lion breaching the TRUST. However the lion proved honorable leaving the group alone. With a full belly he made his departure never to return. This was all done without placing pen to paper. Very little spoken words were needed to make the contract, most of the negotiations took place at a higher level of communication.

For the rest of the journey back to Moonbeams Hopi familiars everything went smoothly. They would arrive in just a few more sun cycles.

The whole tribe was out to greet Moonbeam upon her return. Her parents/birth givers, Souring Eagle and Patch-a-momma could see the new light that Moonbeam brought with her. The whole village would tell the story of Moonbeams journey into adulthood. How she fulfilled her tasks, using her center to speak directly with Gaea.

Not long after her return, Moonbeam with her/our now complete 'spirit group' had their encounter with Maasau. He came from the heavens in a beam of light, appearing to the whole village. Maasau motioned for Moonbeam with her familiars to come with him. They followed him into a cave which opened up into a vast natural cathedral that was close in resemblance to the home that Lazarus welcomed us to at our return to source. Stalactites hung from the ceilings of this great cathedral, with some touching the ground below us like great pillars. Illumination came from out of nowhere as Moonbeam entered. Stories of the universe filled the minds of the 'spirit group'. Our dream vacation "spirit group" shared learned knowledge from our lives as we thanked Moonbeam for sharing her experiences with us.

In this timeline; many events happened different from the timeline that our spirit group of dream vacationers are living in back at the

USE lab in Utopia. The greatest change is with the way society here developed into a civil civilization. Within the teaching of natural law the people learned that we are all familiars/family with a purpose. Conquering armies run by psychopathic logic held little influence in the global mindset. Paying taxes to bullying armies just to keep them from killing was never accepted.

When the Europeans came to Turtle Island/America in this timeline the native Indians never warred with them. The only treaties that were accepted never made a transition from mind to ink with paper. The unnatural greedy bullies that claimed, then took what they wanted, were treated as diseased beings that needed cured. How do you treat a single cell in an organism if that cell believes it is greater than the organism?

We watched from our vantage outside perspective how this timeline handled the arrival of the settlers and the invasion of Turtle Island. Moonbeam journeys were common stories that had been passed down for many generations. Most all knew of the infectious mind disease that had temporality taken hold of the Mayan village, how the village was saved with the return to natural law. Common sense is the sense that we all hold in common with natural law we have to tune all of our senses that we hold in common.

Many of the European arrivals knew natural law because it is part of our heart center, that when touched brings in further recognitions. Once the heart center becomes the guiding force within any being then natural law takes hold. Communication developed with a curing intention. Words with double meanings used to separate class or stature of place someone in illusionary debt slaves were quickly spotted. Many of the settlers had just left behind a land of kings and queens that have formed plantations full of servants called surfs. They are aware how the selfish childlike bullying of these so called monarch caused chaos among the populace. They were escaping from that crazy world of claims with usury forced upon them. This was a fresh start in a new land full of societies that have taken on a more conducive flow with nature. Merit was earned by actions not bloodlines or status.

The ideas of govern-ment developed differently. It was clear that an infectious mindset was encroaching quickly to this new land as some came to make their own claims of rulers in their own empires, being granted by some other conquering bully with twisted selfish intent, giving land away that he has no legitimate claim to. Land grants from conquering armies were laughed into the dustbins as was usury of the native inhabitants or anyone that has found natural law and lives by it.

Orchestration centers were set up in replacement of govern-ments. These centers first concerns is the health of Gaea with the guides in natural law. They brought the four main races together to share knowledge as was designed with the splitting of the races in ancient times. The learned knowledge is used for healing purposes as the concept of war is not even an option. Technology progressed rapidly, as needs arose the answers were always in the genius of the people. Any idea that brought value was nurtured into existence. Profit was not the governing factor in decision making.

Thoughts or ideas can travel faster than anything known to exist. It only takes a willingness to receive information; that comes with not knowing/asking/tuning in.

The other timelines did not live this history/her-story, although the neural network that connects all, now have the spark needed to envision life with a different paradigm.

While we relived Moonbeams journey and timeline our spirit group vacationers played with the concepts that we were being reminded of. Mankind has reached ages of wonder many times with shared wisdom from all over creation. "Civilizations" rise to greatness then eventually fall. In our "prime reality" back in the USE lab our society is on one of those peaks. Can ten million years of learning move man past this hiccup that creates destruction?

...*tim; plummer*...

Our dream vacation was almost over as we decided that our "day" was over and rest was welcomed. More answers to our quest-tions would come to us after a much needed slumber where we will gain a fresh perspective of what we are witnessing.

ALBERT'S JOURNAL OF THE UNIVERSE

14TH ENTRY

DEBT AS SLAVERY

September 2nd-2045
Continued

When we woke from our "dream slumber" we all felt refreshed. Our quest for a cosmic solution to destructive cycles of civilizations would take us on a different path. Our quest was not just for mankind but for all life. Man is not the first to go on this quest. In fact our journey takes us across the universe to a planet called Draction that is ruled by State Government that control the minds of the populace.

This was hard for us to observe without intervention. We choose to ride out our path to see what answers it had to our quest-tions. Instead of self-rule with learned knowledge we were witnessing State rule with ignorance promotion. This was much like Earth so we could not judge. It may sound like rambling as I describe the life on Draction; this is unintentional. Part of this quest we have playfully chosen to travel is looking at planetary consciousness.

The STATE was a construct of the minds that did not truly exist without the energy of the Dractions. Everything was twisted to justify the need for the STATE. The true energy was in the belief of the STATE coming from the populace. Buildings were built that could be called STATE buildings but they sat dormant without the energy of life given to them. The STATE had to be validated to exist at all.

Do to early programming of the people, the STATE was provided energy. Many even thought that the STATE was real and that the existence of the STATE could be proven in the documents that could be provided.

A form of free range slavery was forged by the STATE; all born within the STATE are subject to the STATES care, so a debt is formed that must be repaid with the use of your energy or consent to the STATE validation. Each being is counted then monetized for the STATES benefit as you unknowingly give validity to the STATE as an infant. The STATE takes your energy and eventually lends a small portion of that monetized energy back to the individual as a debtor when he is in fact the original creditor.

Even on Earth we had never seen this level of STATEHOOD. Everything from birth to death was controlled by this illusion called the STATE. The STATE was brought to life by capturing all the spirits at birth. The STATE agreed that land, air or water could not be owned by beings but they could own the land because the STATE is a mind construct with no real validity than ownership. A fiction could own, 'another fiction'. A fiction cannot own a fact but a fact must claim/give energy/validate a fiction to make the fiction real. What logic! The price of claiming ownership is the seizure of property by the STATE. Taxes need to be paid to the STATE so they have the resources needed to police the STATES statutes.

What made this different from Earth is the level of acceptance to the STATE. No one even questions the authority of the STATE. It is as if all concepts created in the neural pathways that make up the universe were being intercepted or manipulated to fit a ruling agenda. No literature was being created, music was rare, and inspiration was stifled. Only STATE sponsored thoughts, creations or ideas made it out to the populace. All marketing was controlled by the STATE filtering everything; you must get STATE approval to do anything creative.

Everything was owed to the STATE. The STATE claimed ownership of language, words, meanings, usage, script or whatever you learn you owe to the STATE. When the question arose about land ownership the STATES reply was that they did not own the land only the title to the land with all improvements made on the land. The STATE is one big plantation, not like on Earth with many ruling plantations; all seeking dominance. Maybe this is the reason for mass acceptance; the populace of Draction has only one master mind group.

The STATE is immortal so mortals are controlled in life as well as death by the STATE. Your children belong to the STATE, the STATE is benevolent; it allows you to live.

The STATE is continually adjusting to the will of the populace or the STATE is a reflection of the will of the people. If the populace wants to be ruled with an iron fist; so be it! That is how they justify agendas. The STATE has many agents, in fact everyone is an agent of the STATE.

How do we take this bit of information? We are all agents of the state of shared existence. Who or what determines the will of the populace anywhere? The state of mind we are in as individuals affects the state of mind in society. If we accept one STATE of being over our state of being do we create a freer state of being or do we capture imagination? If it takes one Master Mind to orchestrate society who or what should make up this Master Mind? Can the state of society's group mind flourish with or without a source of direction?

Man has talked about having a world government. That was actually achieved on Earth for quite a while in our 'prime reality'. Now in our 'prime reality' all of Earths' known resources are mapped on a central world computer with the information available to everyone. Management of the Earths' resources is handled in a way that creates abundance for all. This is done by the world computer and a team of managers. The TRUST is in the technology along with a group of heart centered men/women with the watchful eyes of all. With open dialog for input we have come up with a system that involves everyone. The state of individual being is now a major part of the world mind or state.

We observed Draction further; kind of a behind the scene investigation to find the hidden hand orchestrating the STATE.

The STATE was created by a Draction council of supposed representatives from all corners of their globe. The original intent of the STATE was wonderful. The genius behind the original design of the STATE's by-laws had surprising wisdom of natural law, however written laws are subject to interpretation. Who the laws apply to are subject to consent?

What happens with the tools is up to the holder of the tool. The original STATE created tools that if handled correctly would bring growth and prosperity to all beings. However; in the wrong hand could become a leverage that would drive the Dractions to nothing better than debt slaves to an illusion?

The original STATE trust agreement had due consideration for all within the trust, it also allowed for choice to enter or leave the trust with full comprehension. All would benefit in this original TRUST agreement that formed the STATE.

Even on Draction it took TRUST to create. With TRUST they created a fiction called the STATE. The means in which the TRUSTEES carry out the intent of the TRUST is subject to interpretation. For many generations the Dractions prospered with the TRUST gaining validity with the populace. New generations did not know life without the STATE. Most all were pleased with the prosperity that the STATE shared.

The STATE always provided a stage man to voice the will of the STATE, they even let the populace believe they had a choice in selecting this voice. The face changes at preset intervals although the STATE is run by the same family no matter what face is portrayed.

This is how the Dractions' STATE makes its' claim. When a child is birthed it goes from one (the child which is real) into many making up one (the STATE which is fiction). This is done with registration where the child is given a new name that looks like the given name and a STATE number. The State creates a fiction with the same name as the child written in a different font/letter/symbol. This is where the STATE kidnaps the child as the birth parents give the child away by registering. The parents become the guardians of the child, if the STATE does not like the way you are raising their child, they can take the child away.

The STATE is using TRUST to do all of this, then create a TRUST agreement making the STATE the TRUTEE of the Childs' natural inheritance. With the surety granted by the natural parents and unknowingly by the child; almost unlimited amounts of money can be created for the TRUSTEE to use. The STATE monetizes the surety of the child's lifetime sweat equity times ten with inflation. This credit is used as needed by the TRUSTEE/STATE/MONARCH to fulfill the intent of raising the child to be a productive member of the STATE. The logic is that the STATE owns everything because real beings cannot own anything (even our bodies are on loan). The STATE cannot create it can only capture creations with illusion. Prime creator has GRANTED the STATE the right to become the TRUSTEES of the superior TRUST with nature. They monetize the assets of Mother Nature as well. Using TRUST the STATE gained dominion over everything. No one questioned if the STATE is worthy or in breach of the TRUST. The STATE is not real so those that act for the fiction are living a lie.

The STATE will teach the children what they need to know to become useful to the STATE as a citizen/slave of the STATE. The STATE requires licenses, registrations, permit ion or approval to allow any transactions/transformations of any kind. One must submit to the STATE to do anything to the property that the STATE owns. In reality even the STATE cannot own anything; this is another illusion. The responsibility that comes with ownership is the liability and maintenance. This responsibility was hidden in more trickery making the user/tenant the one holding the bag.

In the original TRUST agreement written by the STATE due consideration was factored into the TRUST (after all the TRUST was set up with the child as BENEFICIARY). As BENEFICIARY each man/woman would reap in the benefits that society provided. Housing along with basic needs was part of the benefits for providing your sweat equity to the STATE. The STATES' prosperity belonged to the living being that helped in the creation, in whatever capacity.

There was never disputes on what philosophy in governance was right or wrong. You could call the structure of the TRUST; Socialism, Communism, or whatever ism you can come up with, it held mutual consideration where everyone lived a good life. This was the original intent of the first STATE TRUST AGREEMENT. How the changes took place, warping the original intent in order to maintain the survival of the STATE is the progressive influence of interpreters.

The interpreters of the original TRUST saw that the benefits of the TRUST were only honorable if the being was living. If a being did not come forward to claim his benefits they were assumed dead so the STATE did not have to honor anything. Once you used your STATE identification you are a fiction/dead/not real and the benefits only apply to the living being. The STATE would then claim salvage rights to abandoned shared profits until the live being proved they existed.

Even those that managed to have their true inheritance honored by the STATE had to follow statutes that if broken could ruin the rightful occupancy of property. A system of harassment usually followed when someone claimed their heritage. The TRUSTEES found a way to control everything taking advantage of any loophole they could find. Many became homeless and desperate as the ones acting in TRUST became wealthy beyond imagination.

Draction became a world of living dead, zombies that acted only for the STATE. The populace on the planet did not even know that all they had to do was replace the TRUSTEES for breach of TRUST, claim their living status then receive their rightful inheritance in a world without debt. Or they could recognize that the real authority was within and even the STATE could not come between you and prime creator/natural law.

Most of the TRUSTEES hid behind even more fictions so no one knew who the living being was that pulled the strings. Each generation became more repressed until the only way to survive was to work for the STATE. Since the STATE controlled the education along with all information available the odds of anyone remembering the original TRUST intent was slim to none.

History/her-story was re-written to make the STATE the Supreme Being that always saves everyone.

On top of stealing the life sweat equity from the beings then making them debt slaves, the STATE began taxing everything. They even charged for any utilities that would not have been possible if not for the gifted then monetized sweat equity of the populace. Everything that nature did not provide freely was prepaid yet they were charging. All roads and infrastructure were charging fools money. The TRUSTEES called it fools money because it had no value yet the populace worshiped it like it was a deity.

The STATE TRUSTEES started separation campaigns by creating names for unique characteristics in looks, thoughts, color, background or whatever could separate. The logic was to keep the populace focused on each other while the TRUSTEES ran away with everything.

...tim; plummer...

Entertainment was provided as distraction also (keep your eyes on the right hand so you do not see what the left hand is doing). Take from others slowly so they do not notice the changes, take advantage of every crisis especially the ones you create.

Was the social programming of the beings on Draction to entrenched for real growth to start blossoming? Without intervention this would only get worse. How do we help a world when we have sworn only to observe. It would only take one neuron of cosmic information to enter the right being for change to begin. We watched as the Dractions gained technology to travel to the stars setting up more TRUST to be broken and manipulated. It was even easier on unsuspecting worlds with abundance of resources. The Beings of Draction became known as Draconians while they spread their dominance across the universe. The Draconians were among the ancient star beings that helped colonize the Earth that we know.

With hundreds of thousands of Earth years perfecting the Draconian system of control they had TRUST agreements pretty much figured out as a way to take control. On Earth it was even easier as the Draconians were like GODS to early man.

Mixed intervention from a multiple of star travelers kept the Draconians from gaining dominance until off world interference was agreed to be stopped, giving the Earth a chance to develop on its own. The Draconians trained feeble minded natives in their art of control convincing these easily duped being into believing they had divine rights.

The Draconians set the stage for their return before de-parting Earth space. The spawns from the seeds that were planted on Earth slowly grabbed hold as Draconians ways spread on a now abandoned Earth.

The Draconians have developed further in the past ten thousand years. They have come to realize the futile destruction that mass control causes, also assuming divinity has repercussions within natural law. This awareness started on Earth before the great star being exoduses. That story is what we witnessed next shared in this journal.

Our spirit group of dream vacationers all have gems of thoughts that will lead to answers in our quest. With the combined knowledge of all of us finally remembering 'all of our previous lives as well as the cosmic mission we are on' we have already found hints that will lead to what we already know. Our thoughts will have to wait as the story continues. This story starts just before the sinking of Atlantis caused by the great flood.

Many of the star visitors on Earth at that time had little knowledge of the Draconian methods of enslavement. Count could not get the more enlightened beings to fall for the STATES claims or TRUST agreements. This world would be easy to dominate as far as the native inhabitants but harder with the star beings intervention. His mission was clear as was his mode of operation; produce value for the STATE using TRUST as a wedge to tip the scales of control. Take truth and turn it into false.

Here on Earth they lived much longer than man does; they were almost immortal by Earth standards living for nine to ten thousand Earth years. The High Councilor for the STATE of Dracion on Earth was a being called Count. Count was the first to arrive on Earth to start colonization reformation. Thousands of worlds were now governed by the STATE so Earth was just a remote colony with little interest. As long as the STATE got their value every two hundred and fifty years they stayed clear, except rarely to visit.

After over a thousand years on Earth the STATE was still the biggest shark in the Draconian belief system. Count had varying degrees of success with his mission. He was not welcome with the galactic gatherings, although he would show up at critical times. Some galactic intervention was needed on more than one occasion as Count stepped way beyond contact protocols. Count agreed to leave Earth with the rest of the star visitors although he had different reasons than what was intended. The star beings stood in his way in completing his mission and with them gone he could convert Earth without interference, he could do better from a distance leaving behind emissaries/pawns to create the STATE. His name became a title for his pawns. His most loyal subjects would be called 'Counts'. Count would share his blood with his loyal pawns giving them longevity along with other abilities that man had but did not develop. This was to give them an edge over other men/women on Earth/Gaea.

Before Count left Earth in his minions control, he saw the most beautiful being he had ever encountered. This being was a hybrid of man and Andromedan. She had an aura that attracted energy like a cosmic black hole. Counts' only desire was to be close to this being that caused feelings within him that he was not familiar with. She was known as Lilly for her radiant beauty. Lilly would bring change to Count that would reverberate all the way to the highest levels of the illusion called the STATE.

With a new/unfamiliar energy Count would help bring about a Macro paradigm shift in thinking. Check the next Journal entry for more of this story.

ALBERT'S JOURNAL OF THE UNIVERSE

15TH ENTRY

COSMIC PARADIGM TRANSFORMATION

September 2nd-2045
Continued

While the Earth developed into a micro cosmism of the macro universe, changes took place that Earth was isolated from. These changes started on a small level although it blossomed then spread its neural pollen across the expanse like a big bang. In order for Count to get close to Lilly he had to adjust his whole mind comprehensions'  or paradigm. Lilly loved being; nothing came between Lilly and source creator, so the idea of the STATE was a comical shame.

Lilly worked well with others whose intention was raising source awareness in all beings. Placing a fiction/lie above The Source Creator was a crime against natural law. This TRUST agreement that the Draconians believed in was against natural order. It became Lilly's mission to show Count the errors in the TRUST. She would encourage Count to return to Source by shutting off learned internal dialog, then taking many perspectives when assessing life questions.

Count used every angle he could think of to just-ti-fy the need for the STATE or some governing authority. "One is born into many that become one", "that is the natural flow in life".

Lilly would reply; "a single cell is born as a blood cell or a bone cell and it does not need a governing authority to fulfill its purpose in life". "If that cell has consciousness of its existence, purpose and the whole creator being that the cell was created for, then they also have will". "The source that created us has given us the ability to choose how we benefit the natural state of the one source creation, if we take that away from others then we are stealing from source needs that will make everything healthier". "The state of the one is made up of the many so we have to make sure that the state of the one is healthy, guided by 'Prime Source Creation' where the energy originated". When your STATE comes between the energy that was created by and for Source they are stealing".

"The purpose for fictions in society is needed whether it be the STATE or some other construct of conscious beings"; Count would respond. "Everything would be chaotic in anarchy if not for a ruling master mind".

"Chaos is a harsh lesson that is sometimes necessary", Lilly conversed gently to Count. "Anarchy is just a society without STATE that has to form a natural state". "That natural state may be chaotic for a while as order will arise with the know-ledge of natural law from Prime Creation". "Fictions are false, the only purpose for fictions is entertainment at best". "Fictions show us facts as they are but shadows of facts". "Fictions are creations of beings so a fiction can never rule over its creator". "You know in your heart that this is true, search within your heart center, do not take my words as truth".

Count took Lilly's advice that lead him on a quest similar to the quest we are on, exploring reality from many different perspectives. Many believed that Count did not have a heart, the truth is that his heart beat was so slow that it was nearly undetectable. His mind worked much quicker than his heart so it took great concentration to center himself. Once this new resource was tapped he flowed with source wisdom. His desire to own and rule seamed to transform into an energy for awareness.

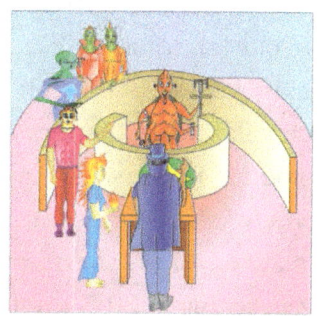

The transformation did not happen quickly, it took thousands of Earth years for Count to come to some areas of awareness then it took a few thousand years for Draction to start back on the path to source instead of a path to STATE.

Meanwhile Draconian programing was reaching new levels on the now abandoned Earth. Draconian ideology took on many forms. Without the one STATE to fall behind, many STATES were created. Almost two hundred STATES were formed as the Earth developed. STATES went to battle with each other using the actual beings/real/live/men/women to fight and die for them. Each STATE had its own TRUSTEES that created their own TRUST with the people. What they all had in common was the STATE always benefited above the people. The Chief Executive Officer or C.E.O. of each STATE represented the STATE or special interest and not the people who created the STATES. Instead of one global monster/creation/fiction/illusion Earth had many monsters/creations/fictions/illusions. Over time this became the natural way of life that is rarely questioned. Loyalty to the STATE was through trickery, fraud, force, coercion, ignorance even implausible deniability. The only state that was made up of natural conscious beings in a group using natural law, was indigenous tribes scattered across the world. These groups were almost extinguished by the TRUST manipulation of the Draconian legacy.

You cannot crush/kill an ideal/idea/thought/neuron/concept, it only transforms, like energy. The dreams of a healthy and better existence as co-creators of reality can only be accomplished with singular/micro awareness of the actual Macro (Prime Creation) with nothing in between. Any constructs of man are to serve man and not vise/versa. It took a while for Macro consciousness shift to finally take place on Earth as Draconian beliefs were no longer accepted after the awakening in 2013 through 2017. The people of Earth took back their energy from any STATE as people finally started acting as stewards of Earth instead of owners. A new state was formed that could not create then rule over debt slaves. Just by not excepting the STATE any longer created a state in man's consciousness.

Chaos did set in after the demise of all STATES rule over live beings stopped. It took a long time for many to grasp that man had to self-govern or control their own minds without attaching on to some kind of STATE control or debt slavery. Out of that chaos came order in a form/likeness never seen or tried on Earth on a global scale. Mans gathered knowledge became available to all, ideas were shared where credit was given to the ones that brought their energy to create anything without claims of ownership. Mutual ownership was even rejected, as 'use' laws were clear in unwritten natural law. To write down natural law is to break natural law, it is considered infringement of Prime Creations copy rights. You cannot claim natural law only use it. Interpretations of natural law was written although there was always a disclaimer statement giving rights to further interpretations. No one argued natural law because a fact cannot be disputed.

The concept behind groups forming states changed; instead of joining groups then having to follow group rule of a mini STATE, we were only joining efforts not groups/clubs/fictions/corporations with authority. Again it took self-awareness of our natural family of man to bring about this change. Education changed as well, children were taught how to think as well as gather information. Natural law is no longer a secret that only a few know, it is taught to everyone. With natural law, violations of each other almost stopped. Violators of natural law suffered isolation as awareness grew.

The person/fiction that was created/captured by any STATE was naturally returned to the live man/woman as the illusion un-veiled. This brought wealth and prosperity to everyone healing Earth/Gaea/Gaia. Fictions became tools instead of governing/mind controllers. The U.S.E. project is a prime example of how this new paradigm/way of thinking has worked for all to benefit. We all work/play for the benefit of all being.

These inserts are summaries of our 'spirit group' thoughts/reflections of the events we are witnessing. We are not active participants in the events being displayed so this is like all of us going to a movie. Back to the movie!

Count finally earned Lilly's love and attention by acting as his own being for the greater benefit all being/source/creation. Lilly's love birthed a new story, Count and Lilly together became a force of nature. They naturally drew the attention of all that they encountered. An intent was formed to undo on Earth the damage that Count left behind as a legacy. Direct intervention was still against natural law although the galactic council provides ways to indirectly help undo past discursions or re-do, atone for mistakes.

Earth was on a trajectory that would pass through a photon belt of pure cosmic consciousness emanating from source. In Earths year of 2012 the pass will begin, Earth beings have legends about this although speculation/interpretation/conjecture/perspective created theories that would prove to be incorrect. Count and Lilly would help the Earth beings take full advantage of this gift from source. In some, time-lines mankind's robotic sleep state it would prove to be a challenge.

The goal for Count and Lilly was to help this occur in all time streams, some would prove to be easier than others. Some, time-streams did not get infected by Draconian ways while others were so entrenched in the beliefs that they are still expecting the return of the Draction STATE. All time-streams will pass through the same photon belt although they knew that there would be a varying degree of success.

Certain beings existed on Earth in all timelines that have a self-recognized connection with source creation that follow natural law. Some kind of spark may need to happen for these beings to speak out. Many of these beings are captured by some STATE. Even if they speak out most STATES will spin events in their favor.

Count was beginning to realize the extent of the damage he and Draconian ways affected source creation on many levels. He became more determined than ever to right this wrong he had perpetrated. Lilly suggested a neural pulse be placed in the Akashi records that could be sent to all of these special Earth beings at once in all time-streams. A consciousness pulse as a precursor to the consciousness wave, a taste of what is coming sent directly to those open to receiving the pulse or message. This could only be done from the Omni-verse where the Akashi records are recorded.

Many layers of source creations were being un-veiled to Count. He could not enter the Omni-verse without reaching a mind in balance with creation, Lilly was his ticket in along with his intent. He was obviously always part of the Omni-verse in any mindset, now he was aware of the stage we are all on which is part of something even greater. For the first time he fully comprehended how a state could/should operate without a STATE. This is what the STATE blocks beings from achieving.

On the Earth calendar the day 11/11/2011 the pulse was sent. Count and Lilly watched for indications that the pulse was received and how the pulse would be interpreted. For those in tune on Earth it came to them as an 'auh-ha' moment, where answers come easily. Questions that only a few people asked started being asked by more. Easy, off the cuff responses from main stream sources was taken with skepticism.

Pleased with the results of the consciousness pulse the next move for Count and Lilly was astral contact within dreams and meditations. Many other star beings started taking a renewed interest in Earth. Most were stunned at the change in both the Draconians and the Reptilians. Their old arrogant posture was now tapered with wisdom, experience and compassion. The galactic council was together in agreement to provide limited help or support, although contact had already increased on Earth after man stumbled on the secrets of the atom.

Count was impressed with the progress of mankind although he noticed that with all the technological advances, man was still in a slave mentality. If man began space travel they would just spread their slave society, infecting the universe again with un-natural lies and deceit. He was depicted by man as a blood sucking parasite called Count Dracula while man practiced every means of control that Count had taught man before his departure and transformation.

The society that man had created had bits and pieces of all the departed star visitors philosophy as well as DNA. For the past three thousand Earth years' man has mimicked the star beings that they remembered. Earth was like a micro-verse shadowing the macro-universe. The macro has gone through transformations that are just reaching the blue marble called Earth. "As above, so below". Changes that took the macro hundreds of thousands of cycles are taking place on Earth in just a couple decades.

Each star group contributed in Earths revival in some capacity. The Moon was still used as a base observatory. Inside the Moon bustled with activity. Lilly and Count set up temporary residence in the Moon. They visited Earth in mans' dreams where man mind was in an alpha state. Mankind started piecing together the cosmic puzzle as information spread when discoveries were made.

The photon belt of cosmic source love energy that began in 2012 on Earths' calendar lasted for decades unlike the pulse that Lilly and Count sent. Looking at life from a micro perspective, things did not change as quickly as observation from the macro. On a micro level, man continued about their daily routines that made up reality for them. Big life changing events went unnoticed by many as a struggle for authority over mankind went into an all-out spiritual battle. This war took place between the 'so called leaders' as well as within them. Like Count, these beings had to see their errors along with the damage that is created by their actions.

Lilly was the incentive for the Count to even consider change. The incentive for the 'want to be controllers' on Earth had to be formed. The source of energy coming from the people had to be severed to create this incentive. The masses of humanity started awakening, seeing behavioral patterns within governing institutions. The bullying/psychopathic/destructive behavior is an illness needing cured. In 2021 a campaign of non-acceptance to harmful actions was ignited, the minions for the controllers that relied on pay checks finally started realizing just how far they had sold their spirits/souls/minds/energy and for such a small price. Inner heart centered guidance/governance was taking control over on a micro level that affected the state of the macro.

Psychological maneuvers that had always worked for hundreds if not thousands of years' no longer swayed man in the direction intended. Corralling the crowds' way of thinking with manufactured events or spinning natural events was not working on an awakened society. Man was no longer worshipping profit as a divine being.

The events we are witnessing are events that most of our group lived through. The perspectives that Count shared is from a macro level. Reliving current events from a new vantage point has sparked insights within our quest. Scout was the first to open up with his insights. "As mice we were totally unaware of the complexities that make up mans' 'made up' world". "We have never had social structures ruling over us accept for man when he captured us". "When one of us got captured by man we became subjects to the will of our captures". "If they wanted us to run through a maze they would take us from a cage, place us in a maze with a piece of cheese as a prize at the end of the maze". "We had no idea that man was doing the same thing to his fellow man". "There is only one path in the maze that we can navigate although another solution slips by us, taking the easy path, up and over the maze".

"The maze that man was captured in only has mental walls created by mind manipulations". Bill began with his thoughts; "in order to solve the maze you must first see the maze for what it is". "The maze is designed to have only one path using our normal senses, if you stray off the designed path you were quickly herded back by your peers". "Man finally solved the maze by realizing that it did not really exist, it was like realizing that Santa Claus was not real or seeing the energy that makes Santa appear to be real". "The long robes that dress a person up to be a judge for a STATE that is not real was taken as seriously as the Easter Bunny". "Role playing for fictions is now comical relief instead of a fearful response". "The monster under the bed that nobody ever sees, called the STATE of whatever, was revealed as the hoax that it was".

"Those that gave all of their energy to the fiction felt foolish once they realized that they were just actors performing character roles for a mirage of what is actually real". Myra opened up; "children stopped lining up to sit on Santa's' lap". "Santa just went away after that leaving behind the spirit/energy of sharing that he represented". "The only thing that made Santa real was belief, only man can believe something into reality that is false". "What man cannot do is produce Santa for all to see/hear/touch without dressing someone up as Santa". "The truth was better than the fictions anyway, it is better to teach the children the truth about giving and receiving and that Christmas is all year long with a reminder once a year".

"Truth is taught to our children now as well as kindling the search for truth in them".

"People love fiction/imagination, it is what makes us co-creators, placing what we create above what created us, is beyond insanity, yet it was accepted by most people". Mary spoke about natural laws of creation; "as a child the magic in the fiction world was fun and exciting". "This dream vacation is just a fabric weaved into being, a fictitious world, a hologram program from our minds memories". "As co-creators we are Prime Creations way of realize and improving on creation". "Witnessing the many stories we have on this shared dream vacation has been wonderful, every story/experience we had, shared a common denominator, struggle for equitable co-existence or a healthier universe". "We have viewed a glimpse of alternate realities, multiple time streams, thousands of past lives, galactic interrelationships we even got glimpses of the Omni-verse, our answers are in us". "We have one more dream day before returning to 'Prime Reality'". "Let's rest for our next journey".

ALBERT'S JOURNAL OF THE UNIVERSE

16TH ENTRY

UNSUPPORTED VALIDATION

September 2nd-2045
Continued

Recapitulating our shared dream experiences has focused us towards finding ways to create new healthier cycles for Source Creation to experience. Looking at our dreams has shown us that there are countless perspectives with even more possibilities. The Draconian Count showed us the follies of living for a corporate STATE. The legends of Count Dracula was a way for the STATE to show how they operate without admitting anything. We are not sure of the intentions of the creators of DRACULA, the mode of operation is the same as the STATE. Both are fictions, both need your consent to enter your house (usually done through trickery), both have no true reflections, both drain your life blood leaving only what you need to live for them, both operate in shadows or through proxy, both expand their domain by creating more vampires and the similarities seem endless.

Studied scholars have just started asking the right questions such as; what is best while we are here or how can we do better? These questions are looked at from a micro/macro level, along with every level in between, above or below. The fractal garden universe is easier to vision than see, hear or touch. The idea that all time exist in each moment is realized with fractal visions. What happens on a micro level happens in the macro and vice versa.

In our sojourns we have glimpsed the fractal garden from the Omni verse. What is beyond the Omni verse can be pondered by observing the micro verse. Bill almost got lost in a fractal journey; even if he feels sure he would have found his way by entering the micro black hole. The vastness/complexities/details of a fractal is governed by Source Creation, shaped by harmonics, bathed in photons of light. The all too real shared hologram that we live in is governed by natural laws that will bring about civilization with extended periods of enlightenment, benefiting Source. Our agreed quest on this shared dream journey is to find these answers.

The knowledge of natural law makes us all Servant Kings/Queens with Source as our benefactor. Source is the original GRANTOR for everything, we must act as TRUSTEES/Servants to the Supreme Trust for existence to be the Beneficiary, making life better for all. As Kings/Queens we have free will with no-one above us. Bringing harm to other Kings/Queens violates natural law; a breach of the Superior Trust with Source Creation.

One could debate that what happened next on this shared dream vacation is beyond comprehension. This story/journal may cause epic skepticism, although with an open heart/mind you will find this easier to follow. The story helps make our answers fun and interesting.

When we woke from our dream slumber we were back in Pangaea with Lazarus and his family. Long lost friends and family greeted us also, spirits/energy/souls that we had not seen since they departed. So many kindred spirits that it would take pages to name them; some of them had new lives with new names, they visiting in a dream state. They were all aware of our adventures in this shared dream vacation, as if they were with us all along. We met with multiple versions of ourselves having the same experience we are having. This was a meeting of minds like no other. No introductions were needed, we recognized ourselves. We came from alternate time-streams, fractal universes as well as different dimensions.

They also knew that our dream journey was coming to a close. We are returning to a world of marvelous potential, mankind is in a golden age like never before. The continual rise in mans' wisdom has brought about the opportunity to co-create on a cosmic, multi-dimensional plane. What an occasion? The sustainability of this wonderful society is the guiding purpose/intent of everyone.

The world tour of the Gateway has allowed man to tap inner potential. What would once be considered child fiction, is now a part of life? Innate abilities like our group developed with the Gateway activations has blossomed into a world of super beings. Adjusting to these abilities is the challenge that man faces. Working together mankind will rise even higher, bonding the relationship with Source. The natural state that is created will bring order resulting in prosperity and abundance.

The formula that was used to gain control (pre conceived solution + create problem + desired reaction = implemented solution) has been recognized and adjusted for the sovereign. This formula was used on all TRUST agreements in history/her-story. The formula for the sovereign is (potential probabilities + focused heart/mind + creative genius + willful action = solution). This is the formula that we follow in completing our quest.

The 'potential probabilities' for our world of advanced man is limitless, it is not our intent to address any or all probabilities, the rest of the formula allows for anything. This intent leads us to the story we witness next.

Our extended group all participated in observing this story. Vision billions of spirits/souls/beings meeting together in the higher dimensions, imagine that they are all versions of you and your familiars with the same intent/focus, they are you. See/feel the energy of love being generated, know that they all hold a key part to answers we are asking. Look around this fantasy landscape of dreams. Enjoy the beauty of what your heart/mind creates. Take every cell making up your existence with us to a quiet little village in Southeast Africa where a child wakes up in a world he is not familiar with.

Delos stretched his arms while looking out his window to the world. The scene was familiar with only the rising sun showing colors through the dew formed on the trees and plants, reflecting light. This would quickly evaporate causing the spectacle to vanish so Delos loved that moment of splendor. Gifts from Gaea, is what he called these moments.

Even at the young age of twelve Delos had a focus on natural reality. He was no stranger to technology either. He was an indigo star child with crystal star children characteristics. In other words he had a knack for learning with technology while having empathy, telepathy and compassion. These crystal characteristics were developed living with his family. He is the youngest in a family of twelve. With six brothers, three sisters and his loving parents they had a full house.

After breakfast with his family Delos went out to play. He was bigger than most children his age, he met with his best friend Anson who was half his size in stature with the energy equal to a bouncing super ball. They would meet Charisma at the village trade market then off to swim in Crystal Lake. The village considered Delos and his friend's young adults at twelve years old, well into their age of reasoning.

The village is located in a valley surrounded by large mountains to the north and west. The mountains to the east are not as large but they are treacherous to navigate. The southern direction was the only easy way in or out of the valley. The valley is large with many villages beside Jackson's village of Willogway. Wealthy in minerals and vegetation no one in the valley needed help from outside the valley. A well-positioned satellite gave the valley access to the world outside.

Being a child in this pocket landscape had many benefits. The wisdom and acquired knowledge passed from generation to generation had little to no contact with corruption. With nothing to corrode the minds of the people the inhabitants flourished in spiritual growth. [tp1] Thousands of years have passed since a small group from sunken Atlantis migrated and settled in the valley. The existing inhabitants of the valley at that time welcomed them into their hearts. They brought with them language, script along with knowledge of Source Creation. It is said that they came in search of a divine flint that sparked creation.

While swimming, a storm came over them that would bring buckets of water falling from the sky. Delos, Anson and Charisma took refuse under a boulder that balanced on a nearby hill. This boulder had been on this hill as long as anyone could recall, the legends tell how the boulder was placed there by star- beings millions of years ago. For the children it was only shelter from the storm. Streams of mud washed by them as the hill was being rapidly eroded by the torrential rain falling around them. The boulder began to shift, as if would start rolling down the hill. The children were awe struck but in no danger, being on the uphill side of the spherical boulder. The boulder moved about five feet then stopped as if it was moved intentionally.

The newly exposed Earth had the shape of a granite vortex that was just big enough for the children to enter. A cloud of gas came out of the vortex that could be seen even in the pouring rain. The gas took on the likeness of a man then rose into the skies, the rain stopped at once. Delos, Anson and Charisma were so close to the vortex that they all breathed in some of the gas. They ran into the village telling everyone their story. When they returned with the villagers the boulder was back in place as if it had never moved.

The villagers all agreed how strange it was that the storm came on so suddenly then stopped just as quick. Evidence of the rest of the children's story could not support what they said. Mud was washed away with a lot of erosion exposing the base of the spherical boulder but known alignments along with accurate demographics of the valley's topography showed no substantial change. There were no marks on the earth indicating a shift.

Delos, Anson and Charisma went home convinced they had imagined much of the days' events. Jackson looked on his computer for spherical boulder to find out if there were other such rocks or boulders around the planet. To his surprise there were many thousands reported spherical rocks found around the world. There was just as many stories/legends/theories as there were reports of findings. None of the information reported indicated that the rock have ever moved without outside influence. One theory that caught Delos' imagination was that the boulders were blocking portholes to other dimensions.

He went to sleep with his mind racing with possibilities. In his dreams he meets up with Anson and Charisma again. Together they travel to other societies around the globe. Splendor was mixed with destitution, imbalance of Gaea's gifts were painfully clear to these sheltered children with unchallenged empathy. The three children were confused by the suffering they felt as they merged with the state of mans' group consciousness. Delos woke in a rush having full recollection of his vivid dream. It was still dark out so Delos got back on the internet to confirm what he already knew to be true. This was the year 1997; how could a civilization become so imbalanced? This was not like his life in the valley.

Here in the valley there is no monetary system or exchanges of currency/money. This stood out to Delos as he reviewed his memories of his dream. Money systems existed throughout the world at every level except for the money creators who trade the value of Gaea (which belongs to everyone) and the sweat equity of people using funny money. In our valley we function as one with all wealth or prosperity shared equally as we recognize the roles we all play in making life better for all. The valley has many aqua grow domes that specialize in herbs, spices, exotic fruits or vegetables. As children we are taught how the balance system works in our society and we choose how we help in the process.

Crimes against each other almost never occurs because we all have what we need to not only survive but thrive. Watching people (in his dream) who have brought value to the world end up with nothing is a crime in natural law. That was hard for Delos to comprehend because this does not happen in the valley

Fruit trees and vegetable gardens are part of our landscape and free for all (provided by Gaea and our loving attention). Even the preservation and processing is done by those that love creating with what man and nature produced. There is a planning and organization group although they cannot make it happen without the energy of the people so they are not placed in a higher standing that the ones that clean up or help in any other capacity. Trade with those outside the valley was not done with money either, the valley traded surplus from harvest along with products developed or produced by the people. In returns they got other items of value that belonged to the people, not the ones making the exchanges. We have kept up with technology and even contributed in this field through our higher learning fields of study.

I guess you would say that everything is free in the valley although that is not how we look at it. We have learned from nature that we all have to take action to make life better for all. The bees all work together to create the bee hive, without a payday of perishable tokens. The bees do not classify themselves as Communist or Democratic or whatever yet they all have a hive to live in as they work together to feed each other. As people we are not stuck with the hive mind, we can reach beyond the hive while still helping the 'state' of the hive. Nothing is free, it is already paid for with past sweat equity that has already been paid, raw materials were provided by nature, so we owe nature a debt that we pay with our care for nature. We are all taught to give back freely what is given freely.

It became clear to Delos how wise his ancestors were when planning the development of the valley. The history/her-story of the valley tells how the Atlantis people that migrated into the valley brought with them knowledge from the universe along with a great comprehension of Natural Law. We are all descended from these migrants here in the valley. We developed virtually unaffected by outside influence.

The valley was never invaded by conquering psychopaths being impossible to move an army into the valley. As a result no taxes have ever been imposed on any people or a need for money ever existed. The only competition that is encouraged in the valley is with yourself. "Always strive to improve"; that is what we are encouraged. Winning was a sense of accomplishment and losing (or not getting the desired result from effort) was a lesson to do better.

They taught about the follies in the outside world in Delos's curriculum and access to global information is readily accessible to all living in the valley. Experiencing these follies in his dream was intense, looking with empathy brought clarity. This was his first real experience with emotions he had never felt, such as fear, despair, hunger, anger, jealousy, coveting, and brutality.

Later while sharing his dream with Anson and Charisma they discover that they all shared the same dream. Anson paced the rest of the evening and Charisma cried after waking. Now they had more secrets that they could not share with anyone else. Anson bounced around like a jumping bean and one of his springs left him hanging on to the top branches of a nearby tree. Anson's only response was; how cool was that?

Charisma was so surprised that she began to look like the gas we breathed in, she floated up to Anson with hardly a thought. With both his friends stuck in a tree Jackson stayed grounded, he wondered if he was still sleeping and he was grateful that no one saw this happen.

Anson and Charisma climbed down the tree the hard way, branch by branch.

There was more happening here than the three children could grasp. The excitement continued when they reached ground level. Being children with wild imaginations they played with ideas of what costumes they could wear and what their names would be as super heroes? Anson wanted to be 'Kid Kinetic' and Charisma wanted to be called 'Ether'. Delos felt like a third wheel with no abilities showing up. As they played, Delos began to vision Source Creation with a ring side view, he saw how nature was a being, traveling through endless space as part of an even greater whole called the galaxy. Fractal existence was seen as whole.

With a smile that would light a room, Delos said; "and I will be 'Cosmos the Galactic Shaman', my outfit will look like the stars in the heavens".

These children have no idea that we have been observing their story or the relevance their story holds in our quest. We are not sure ourselves yet. Our scene shifts to a seemingly unrelated event that was taking place a few light years from Earth. The Star Ship 'Expedient' from the Orion belt had deployed an exploration cruiser heading out of our galaxy toward our neighboring Andromeda galaxy. This cruiser would have some difficulty when reaching the 'Sol' solar system causing the crew to abandon the cruiser in rescue pods. The quantum energizers were breached by a mini meteor of compressed mass. Upon impact the mass began to expand, the crew had just enough time to abandon the small cruiser. The nearest planet that would support the Orion crew was Earth.

Earth was in a restricted area, quarantined, off limits to all. It has been over four thousand years since the Orion's visited Earth, this exception to the quarantine would strand the crew but save their lives. Earth has two location that would welcome the stranded crew, one was in the land of the Hopi Indians and the other was the Valley in Africa.

The valley was chosen for its remote, hard to reach location. They would have less chance of being detected.

Six cloaked pods entered Earth's atmosphere heading towards the Valley. Once they land the pods will become home for these wayward visitors. No one should be able to see or detect them so they will live out the rest of their existence secluded or until the quarantine on Earth is lifted. They would land in the mountains just north of the Valley completely undetected, or so they thought.

Delos, Anson and Charisma were still at play in an open field in the northern area of the valley. Delos perked up with excitement as the pods past over them approaching their landing. He saw the pods pass over and immediately wanted validation from his friends; "Anson, Charisma, look at the ships".

Neither one of Delos's friends saw anything. This did not stop Jackson from heading into the mountains in the direction he saw them landing. Anson and Charisma followed, just for fun. They believed Delos even if they did not see or hear anything. When the children reached a higher vantage point Delos could see the pods where they docked to Mother Earth; "look! Now do you believe me"? Delos was sure to get their validation now that the pods were in plain sight.

Pointing at a nearby plateau; "See, there are six of them, they look like metallic lady bugs". "Wait! One of them is opening, look! Don't you see"?

With a show of support Anson answers; "if they are there, it is a long way to travel". "Charisma and I may be able to get there quick but you would take half a day at best". "Apparently, your ability is to see what no one else can see". "We will all have to go together".

Charisma was doubtful as she did not see anything or could not see anything now; "it will be dark before we even reach the bottom of this mountain and we cannot climb in the dark". "Our familiars will be worried if we are not back for dinner". "We have so many secrets from them already". "They would not believe us if we told them". "Our abilities must be kept secret also, even if it would help others believe us".

"They may not be there tomorrow"; Delos said in a frustrated voice. "We have to go now, I will go alone if I have to". "I am not imagining this, what I see is clear to me".

Both Delos's friends remembered how it felt when the village did not believe them, they began to doubt themselves. "We better get moving if we are all going"; Charisma said hesitantly. "Our familiars will look for us here first, so we should leave them a message". "My phone is out of range with no signal, we can record a message then leave the phone for them to find".

Anson reached in his knap sack; "here is a flashlight we can leave on so they find the phone quickly" "I will point it to the sky, when it gets dark it will be easy to spot".

After leaving a message the children began their descent leading to their ascent to the plateau. Climbing was second nature to them growing up almost completely surrounded by mountains. They moved stealth fully, helping each other when needed. The terrain was treacherous in places where running streams with slippery rocks made helping each other a necessity. They used all that nature provided to help them, one tree provided a root system that protruded out the side of a steep cliff, allowing the children a faster shortcut to their destination.

The sun was setting and they still had two flashlights. When darkness enveloped the sky with a partial moon and billions of stars, it was spectacular to behold. Charisma became luminescent, lighting up the whole area around them.

"That is a pretty handy ability when you need it"; Anson played kiddingly. "Now everyone will know where we are". "I can hear it now, 'large green luminescent orb was spotted in the mountains just north of Willogway'". "They will be making theories and conjecture about this phenomenon for years".

Charisma giggled; "we could stare our own theories, throwing everyone way off base". "A gathering of fairies or a divine light from source". "A divine light from Source is almost true, we are just leaving out the details".

"It may be best to just keep silent about all of this"; Delos replied, breaking the mood of levity. "Even silence is a lie, although it is better than spoken lies or unbelievable truth". "You two only believe me because we are friends and what we are going through together". "Only I am sure of what I saw".

Delos continued on intently, his purpose was focused. Charisma and Anson were with him the whole way up to the plateau. There was a thick forest greeting them when they reached their goal. The Plateau was larger than it looked from a distance with lush vegetation. It was the middle of the night but Delos knew they were close. Charisma dimmed her luminescence to a small radius to travel through the woods. After a couple hundred yards they came to an overlook into a much smaller valley.

Delos saw the six space ships had landed in a circle. The area was bustling with activity. Pointing at the small valley he looked once again for his friend's validation; "now I know that you can see that".

ALBERT'S JOURNAL OF THE UNIVERSE

17ᵀᴴ ENTRY

TRANSFORMATION EXPECTATION

September 2nd-2045
Continued

When Delos looked at his puzzled friends he knew they did not see anything but a beautiful natural valley. The view was awesome, worth the climb, but there were no spaceships.

"Come on, we have come this far, so humor me a little more". "Let's go into what I see as the belly of the beast". "They may be able to see us, so you do not have to come with me".

With playful excitement Anson responded; "are you joking, we would not miss this for all the tea in China". "Charisma, stop the light show for now". "They came here in stealth mode and so will we". "Over there is a quick way down, come on, what fun".

The children entered the circle of ships with Charisma and Anson giggling playfully. With a serious voice Anson burst out; "greetings space beings, we come in peace".

This was funny to Charisma because there was nothing around but flowers and trees, controlling her laughter; "yes, you, celestial flower of the cosmos, we are addressing you".

"Shhhh"! "Be quiet, they are approaching us": Delos seemed intense. "They see us, we are not in danger, and I feel their surprise"

Charisma and Anson watched as Delos began a conversation with what they saw was just air; "I am the only one that can see you". He spoke as if there was no communication gap between the two species. "My friends think I am seeing things, I see and hear you".

"That is a very lonely path, my dear spirit". The visitor replied to Jackson. "We are here with a strict moral code of non-interference". "You cannot reveal our presence here".

"That is no problem, see how my best companions are reacting in dis-belief". "That is an example of the ridicule I would get". "May I visit you"?

"You and your companions are welcome, none other". "We are stranded here as explorers so you can help us explore your world without our interference". "The decision to remain anomalous is to protect mankind". "Man is on a journey that cannot be interfered with". "We watched you come here, what we did not expect is that you could see or detect us, then again you are not ordinary children". "We exist just outside your vibrational senses, not even your limited technology can pick up our presence". "Tell us how you came by your ability".

Delos shared the story of the sudden rainfall, the spherical boulder, the gas cloud that took the shape of man, the granite vortex under the boulder, the sudden stop of the rain along with the rest of the story leading them to the landing site.

Charisma and Anson just sat down to watch their friend rant at thin air. They were sure he was trying to make up for his lack of a super ability. At the same time they felt Delos' sincerity, knew his integrity and wanted to believe him.

"This entity that you saw leaving the vortex must be the energy we feel around us". "It is a benevolent energy that has been tasked here to help man, this is the being's home planet and he feels the imbalance". "Like us, he is just out of reach to normal senses, he is advanced way beyond mankind". "He chose you children, we will trust his assessment of you". "Somehow this being knew we would be coming and prepared a way for man to contact us". "You can teach your friends how to start seeing us, they have it within them".

"You chose the name 'Cosmos' earlier with your friends. That was a very intuitive choice". "Here is a gift that will show your friends our shared truth, then they will have to reach a point where we can be seen". "To you it looks like a medallion, no one else can even see it". "They will see what it can do, it is called a 'necessitate'. It will provide things that are absolutely necessary upon your command". "Use it sparingly and discretely". "It was our 'necessitate' that saved our lives". "Each of us carries one and now you have one also". "If you find it necessary to know anything, it will provide a variety of knowledge". "All your questions about us will be answered". "Let it hang next to your heart, where the answers are in reality".

The sun was beginning to rise before the children got any rest. The trip back to the Valley got off to a late start. Delos said his farewells to his imaginary/invisible friends from the Orion Belt. He was the one in a playful mode now as Charisma and Anson were worried about their familiars. He told them as much as possible while hiking through the forest. When they reached the edge of the plateau they could just barely see the Valley between two smaller peaks. They watched an eagles' effortless flight across the expanse that would take them hours on the ground. Anson could bounce his way quickly and Charisma could just float there in minutes.

Delos grabbed his invisible medallion thinking how great it would be to fly across between the peeks and right into the Valley. Several possibilities appeared in his mind all at once, he looked around to see what Mother Nature could provide then told his friends to go ahead without him, He would be right behind them. He began visualizing a completed glider using just the branches, leaves, vines and elements around him. He calculated weight, size, distance, airflow, path and risks in a couple seconds then looked around seeing his glider complete,

he strapped in then leaped at just the right moment. The wind picked him right up as he flew passed Anson and Charisma.

"How do you like my glider"? Delos yelled as he flew by them; "I made it from nature".

Both his friends decided not to tell him he was not in a glider, he looked so graceful holding a stick in each hand with his arms stretched out like wings. Maybe there were space beings that he talked to all night?

They were back in the Valley in minutes, landing unnoticed by anyone. Before splitting up to go home they each made a vow of secrecy.

For the next few weeks the children got together every day to practice their abilities and listen to Delos recount his dream journeys. "We all have a purpose with responsibility that comes along with our gifts"; Delos was forming a plan that he wanted his friends part of. "Playing the role of 'Cosmos the Galactic Shaman' is coming naturally to me although my progress is not visible like your abilities". "For now, you will have to be open to what we need to do". "I can only tell you the plan along with the intent, your free will can choose from there".

"As a Shaman, 'healing' is an ingrained passion". "In order to start the process of healing the dis-ease must be traced to its origin". "The big picture is being shown to me in my dream journeys, balance is being restored in the universe and Earth must be a part of that restoration". "The stranded beings from Orion communicate with me all the time,

I wear a headset so others will not think I am too crazy when they see me talking to myself".

Knowing how his friends loved to play, Delos laid out the plan for the playground; "we can call ourselves 'Trinity' or 'Terrific Trinity' or whatever, then go undercover to fight the forces of injustice".

"I like 'Terrific Trinity' as our cover"; Anson loved imagination games. This game has real super powers. "We must remain in the shadows so that a mystery is formed around us". "What is our first mission"?

"Ideas have powers, part of, yet beyond the physical realm". "Our way of life here in the Valley is powerful information for the world to see". "The Valley functions as one living being made up of everything that lives there". "First we must seek out those that have the same ideas, they will show up as we open up". "Together we will be a catalyst that breaks down illusionary control over others".

To the surprise of the children they were approached by an honored wise councilor "Altus" known throughout the valley. As Altus approached, he kindly spoke; "seek and you shall find". "You children have tapped universal forces that will attract alternate reality support, you will light a beacon that will change the dogma of our world". "I am only the first to arrive here, because I am closest in location to you".

"You children and the story you are authoring is being observed by galactic time/space seekers of universal health". "Delos, you may feel their presence"? "They have questions". "Prime Creation has led them here for answers".

How could Altus know we are watching this story unfold? A version of this question tapped most of our dream vacationers at the same moment. However, it was just a passing thought as we continued observing what was unfolding.

"I know they are here with us, along with ancient guiding spirits from all corners of reality"; Delos replied. "I am not sure why"? "I have not shared this, no-one believes me about the stranded Orion explorers, so I am careful with what I share".

"That freak storm was much more than a natural occurrence"; Altus continued. "A worm hole was opened then closed, this was observed by many on an international scale". "This valley is about to be invaded for the very first time since the arrival of the Atlantis settlers". "Scholars, truth seekers, shamans, the Grandmothers, scientist, agencies of governments, indigenous people with ancient knowledge and many, many more are on their way here to the Valley". "Not all will come with positive intent". "They do not know of you children, you may want to keep it that way until you feel that source connection of TRUST".

"The arrival of your Orion friends did not go completely unnoticed either". "Nothing technical picked them up, but many of those that I just mentioned do not use technology as their way of searching the heavens". "Only a few will even be aware of both occurrences". "Most will be focused on the suspected worm hole opening". "This is being de-bunked by the Valley Council". "Even the invasion of well-intended wisdom seekers is not welcome in the minds of the Council". "They would be more open to the Orion explorers than curios man".

As predicted by Altus the Valley began to have many visitors. New stories were created from hearsay, speculation and limited first-hand experience. A number of perspectives became experts in their own view, insisting that the conclusions that they had could be the only answer. Rumors sprang from gossip based on bits and pieces of witnessed events. Living light traveling through the mountains, flying children, moving spherical boulders, space visitors. Multidimensional invasion was the general conclusion, with no real proof.

The children sought out the good intended visitors to offer them the opportunity to join their path to help mass, global enlightenment. The only alien invasion going on was in the mind, as new thoughts, with the potential to void out or nullify past dogmas/paradigms. The path leads man back to natural order without blind slavery to a man-made illusion of outside author-ity. Source Creator is the superior authority and source is within everything, so the higher author is within. Let our miss-takes become reminders of what does not work so we are not destined to repeat them.

To the children; the message was more important than the events that drew the visitors to the Valley. It was agreed that the best way to proceed was to place nuggets of truth out that only the aware would see. Many would pass the nuggets of truth without seeing any value, then some will pick the nugget up and place it in their pouch of learned wisdom (the pouch that can never be full). As people share the nuggets that they find they will tell others how they found this nugget of truth that can never be spent and has endless value, to be shared freely.

The Valley is an example of how mankind can thrive without the slave master called MONEY. That is what stood out to the visitors to the Valley. For thousands of years the people in the Valley have produced abundance without creating a medium means of exchange. This accomplishment was challenged by the programmed visitors as their paper had no value so the illusion of wealth was gone like a puff of smoke. The visitors that did not adjust to the Valley were politely escorted out of the Valley. For those that stayed behind life took on a whole new outlook. The children in the Valley would be considered genius or be punished for non-conformity, depending on the mind lock of the group communities outside the Valley. The thing that was most apparent was the never ending search for learning was in all of the indigenous people in the Valley, how they worked together in their everyday activities. Each person is giving back continuously, making the whole Valley prosper as one being.

This absence of Money was the nemesis to the money creators and money changers. The children had no idea of the kind of mind control they were up against in the outside world. The idea that man can thrive without a profit driven monetary system cannot be allowed to enter the imaginations of the people.

A battle was secretly waged by the money creators as the children spread their nuggets of wisdom. This would become an energy battle that was intended to break the spirit without shedding any blood.

Altus shared his knowledge of the outside world with the enlightened group that was quickly forming around the children. Many changes that would benefit all of mankind were already in the works. This new group of geniuses would support the efforts of all positive action groups around the world.

Our cosmic group of dream vacationers watched as ideas formed that would bring about the change, bringing consciousness to the people of the world. This would spark the age of light we all share back in our "prime reality".

Schools of inner governance spread. These schools inspired students towards the path that provided happiness. They taught natural law at a kindergarten level throughout theirs entire learning process. Natural law is a continual study, so even the masters do not claim superiority. All knowledge was made available. Many versions of history are taught from many perspectives. The Indians of America (Turtle Island) do not share the same story as the conquering settlers with the claim of "Manifest destiny".

Imagination was encouraged as long as no harm resulted from the exploratory minds. Bully behavior that forms the adult psychopath were taught cause and effect or why that behavior would not work in our world of Natural law. Only inner competition was encouraged as completion with others was put in perspective.

On other fronts Altus, Delos, Charisma, and Anson helped bring about self-sustainable communities that traded surplus with other communities. Vegetable gardening returned to the backyard as hydroponic technology became easily accessible and accepted. Neighborhood gardens sprang up all over the place. In the cities, old buildings were converted into multi story growing gardens eliminating the need for large areas of farm land.

Insurance companies started becoming obsolete as people realized how their hard earned sweat equity could be used to invest. Instead of giving away their energy, people learned to make their energy work for them. Community owned clinics, auto repair shops, hospitals, schools even construction crews stared replacing the insurance companies as spiritual currency was used more wisely. This event took the wind out of the world society's illusionary controller's easy path of dominance.

The breach of trust that was taking place within the governments became common knowledge. The nations of the world had to stop their plantation manipulations and return what the stole from the people, to the people. Immigration was finally seen for what it was, a source of revenue for the plantation controllers. Why would a sheep farmer return sheep that he can shear for life? Enticing the sheep into the plantation is part of the plan, while voicing public opinion or stealing the truth from the people.

The Postal service took on a whole new purpose as network specialist. When the teleporter was invented, they were the leaders in setting up teleportation sights everywhere. The Postal service helped re-create the global internet into the group mind that is free to be critical.

Altus, Delos, Charisma, and Anson worked with teams that re-worked the weight and measures into a fair and equitable exchange for all trading parties. They also helped map the resources of the globe, then come up with ways to sustain or renew the resources for future generations to come. This was a mass undertaking that involved all the people of the world one way or another. Nature preservation was the guiding rule so Natural law grew to have more understanding.

The older members of our soul group all had roles we played in bringing about many of these changes. The world that we will return to in 2035 "our prime reality" is a result of these changes. The excitement to return home to "prime reality" was growing as the dream vacation was coming to an end. Altus, Delos, Charisma, and Anson are probably living in our "prime reality, so we could meet them when we return.

...tim; plummer...

Each individual in our "prime Reality" are authoring their own stories for the first time since the ancients. The aggregate society sets up the scenery with the help of the individual. The state of man was now operating without the STATE as a parasite. The left and right hemisphere is now working together as one mind.

ALBERT'S JOURNAL OF THE UNIVERSE

18TH ENTRY

DREAM AWAKENING

September 2nd-2045
Concluded

We all woke up in the USE lab at the same time. Some of our group chose to just lie there and ponder. Bill, Seth and I could not wait to review the monitors. Bill gave the computer the command to replay the activities of the day within the lab environment. Upon reviewing the playback we saw that our soul group did not move much while in our dream slumber. What was going on around our physical bodies was amazing.

At the start of the tape recordings we saw projections of each one of us rise up out of our bodies then disappear. Every so often these astral forms would return then leave again. We determined that these returns were our rest periods. The recordings showed that on many of our return trips we brought with us astral forms that were not a part of our soul group. In fact some of them stayed and are with us still. We all feel the presence of Seth's violet flame Shawna, Zeb, I am and many more.

Scout and Jasmine mice had one of our biggest surprises, Jasmine announces that she is pregnant. In fact, she looks like she is ready to deliver soon. She was not with children when we started our dream journey, this was indeed a miracle. These baby mice are immaculate conceptions as no physical contact that could result in pregnancy took place. A litter of cosmic mice was soon to join us in our "prime reality".

A holographic image of our dreamscape appeared above our resting bodies and changed as our adventure in the fifth dimension progressed. The whole room lit up at times so bright that it became hard to distinguish what was going on. The sharing of these recordings was up to the USE purveyors of information team. This journal will follow. It will not be the same as being with us on the dream vacation although dream vacations soon became common as more learned how to tap the fifth dimension.

It was time to share our experiences as I sat down to compose this journal. All of us would never see life quite the same way that we used to. A whole new world of possibilities have opened up and as part of sustainable health, will remain open.

We compiled a list of what we felt it would take to create a long lasting enlightened civil-ization that would benefit creation.

Create and keep TRUST agreements as individuals with "Prime Creation" or whatever you call your higher being.

The learning and teaching of 'Natural Law', along with the wisdom of our connection to nature.

Keep 'Natural Law' natural, realizing it is an endless study.

Improve existence where or whenever you are, leave a positive imprint. Be creative, yet mindful of cause and effect.

Due consideration of both the micro and the macro.

Do not accept destructive behavior (the phycopath), within or without. Write or Author your own story, guided by your heart/mind.

Do not close the book on any subject. Keep your thirst for knowledge after it has been quenched.

Speak the truth as you view it, even in fear. The truth changes moment to moment.

Validate or consent to only what benefits everyone, without holding your rights above others.

Remember that man's creations are made to serve man, just as we serve creation (our creator and sustainer).

Be heart/mind full. "Nuff said".

The only thing you should judge is whether something is harmful or helpful to life. This is really a choice; not a judgment. Gravitate to what is helpful, even a single cell of our body knows this. "Natural Law"!

Laugh regularly, be happy. This should be higher on this list.

Choose your master and let others choose. Wisdom leads you to your true master within.

This list will con-tinue as we con-jure more con-cepts as nothing is con-crete.

While the adults played with our list, the children (Brandon, Penny and Charles) searched for Delos, Charisma and Anson. They would be adults now and the children wanted to hear more of their story. Brandon found a group called 'Infinite Learning' that was stimulated by Delos, then acted upon by his whole soul group.

Excited about finding the children from their 'Dream Vacation', Penny giggles; "send a note asking if we could meet".

Even more surprising was the quick response to the note, as if they were waiting for the message. They all agreed to meet at a mutual playground to both, the USE building was known well by Delos. Delos, Charisma, Altus and Anson could arrive within a couple hours.

"This meeting alone is proof of our shared journeys together"; Bill pointed out. "It is a wonder that our stories may have common denominators". "Another cosmic reunion".

When the Valley children arrived they were greeted like long lost siblings. Over a dinner that could not be matched, they swapped stories and compared notes. Delos fell in love with the children and the mice tribe along with everyone else. He radiated love in a natural way, they all did.

Our accounts of the dream matched with a few surprises. We were all invited to visit the stranded exploration team from Orion. The bullet train was not necessary because the mind is the fastest way to travel.

With Mary's help we all linked minds again, in moments we were visiting the Orion explorers. They welcomed us as if we were old friends.

"Join us for an evening walk my friends". I am called Otto by your Earthly companion Delos or 'Cosmos' his chosen name. Your world has gone through a great transformation since our arrival here. We now have the means to return to our home planet, although we have made a new home here".

"You Earthier are unique in the galaxy. An accident stranded us here, where and when we were meant to be here. Our people have a history way beyond Earth. When your world was just developing, we visited quite regularly. You mistook us for gods so we gave you nuggets of information, then left you alone to develop on your own".

"In the last two hundred rotations around your sun you have reached a place in the universe of interest. Nowhere in our know existence is a planet with such diversity of life and spirit/energy. Earth is traveling through a photon belt, you have crossed over the event horizon where you aligned with the center of the galaxy". You are aware of this 26,000 year cycle and are asking how to hold on to what you are accomplishing through the downward path in the cycle, thousands of years from now in your time stream".

"By now you have learned that the intent to sustain your civilization has as many possible variables as there are stars in the universe or cells in your bodies. You have learned that all you can do is continuously improve life in the now/present that will naturally prepare you for what may come next, short of something catastrophic".

"You have learned that there is no true beginning but many, many beginnings. Just as there is no end only a new beginning".

"Your quest up until now has shown you how you arrived where you are now. Where you go from here is up to you. Just as the micro shapes the macro, the past shapes the present and the present shapes the future".

"You honor us with your visit. You feel that you have achieved biological immortality although you cannot be sure of that until you wake up the next morning over and over. Maybe a glimpse into the future will tell you if you are immortal. Yet you have seen your immortality on your journey, is this not good enough? Your quest changed to the intent of sustainability as you discover again that in order to sustain you must take care/improve the current state of being continuously.

"We love, laugh and learn with you as you make your discoveries on your seemingly endless quest for source". "We wish you to not only sustain but flourish in the life granted by 'Prime Creation" who TRUSTED you to be here".

Our visit did not last long, although we will visit again. This visit allowed the Orion explorers to make their presence known to the world. They had slowly started mixing with more people, now they are common knowledge.

Before concluding this journal of our dream vacation there is one more event worth mentioning. The photon energy being Shawna that returned with us from our dream vacation manifested into a physical vessel. How this was even possible is still not clear.

The theory is that we are all made of the same elements as the stars so with the help of Charles and Penny they pulled the molecules from the ether that is everywhere to create stem cells. These stem cells multiplied at an alarming rate bathed in sea water while developing inside a life sustaining bubble created by Penny. Myra's essence of healing also helped speed the process as an organic body developed. At just the right moment, the essence photon that is Shawna entered the soul vessel. A strand of her DNA was provided by Seth who kept her close to his heart in a locket hanging from his neck.

Many people kept locks of hair from their loved ones in hopes of bringing them back someday. Cloning a body was achieved many years ago, the trouble was that the cloned body was vacant from the soul/spirit so it was void of consciousness. The cloned bodies were also

missing the divine energy that it takes to keep the heart beating so the clones did not live for very long, Shawna's soul/spirit was with us, making the vessel whole.

This was much different that cloning as it only took a couple hours for the adult figure of Shawna to fully develop. The team effort that it took to make this happen was orchestrated by Myra and Mary.

Bill and I were busy in conversation with Altus, Delos, Anson and Charisma while this was accomplished in the lab we took our vacation in. Seth, Mary, Myra and the children introduced us to the newly born Shawna with Myra saying; "we can now bring back the ones we loved and lost if we can locate them, before they are born again with a blank consciousness state as a baby".

"One just needs to locate the soul/spirit in the upper dimensions, then get the free will choice of the soul to return", Mary added as a re-afferent. "The soul/spirits visit us in our memories and dreams".

The chances for bringing back some of the most ruthless, diabolical characters in history was non-existent because a soul/spirit must reach a stage of conscious enlightenment to allow the return too this physical reality. All soul/spirits have the capacity to reach this enlightenment, as we have witnessed in our journeys. Many of these diabolical spirits were nothing but sock puppets to others that used the psychopath within them.

What you have read here in this journal you may feel is just the wild imaginings of a dreamer. Thank you for that assessment. If you are still reading then I must greet you, recognize your presence by telling you that "I love you".

"You are special if you have fun in this world/story/dream/playground". "I am sorry, please forgive me, thank you and I love you".

"Wait, just a second more". "Keep reading for just a moment more". "The day ended with Jasmine mouse having a litter of twelve mice". "Another impossible mind-blowing event to end our day". "Now I am really testing your imagination, pushing on the walls of knowingness". "What should we name these miracle mice"? "Any ideas are welcome"!

This is Albert, signing off on this day's journal entry. Tomorrow will bring us another adventure, if I do not dream of one tonight.

www.ingramcontent.com/pod-product-compliance
Lightning Source LLC
LaVergne TN
LVHW021951060526
838201LV00049B/1669